Beneath Lies Beauty

Beneath Lies Beauty

By
Jacqueline Collen-Tarrolly

Toadstool Farm Burbank, CA

For All Misfits everywhere.
You know who you are.

Prologue

One thinks of fire as quiet, as the silent flicker of a candle or gas lamp flame, or the soft crackle of a fireplace, but it's not really. Fire roars like a hell spawned beast. It screams and rages and drowns out all sound except for its monstrous destruction. I heard nothing but the fire, not the cries of those trapped, not the shouting of those trying to help, not the crashing of burning curtains and walls coming down, though I knew in my panicked mind that those sounds must be there.

But it was only the fire...and the smoke. There was so much smoke. And the stinging tears that blinded me were starting to dry though the coughing was getting worse. I thought briefly that this could not be a good sign. God, I couldn't see. I couldn't breathe. Some blind instinct was pulling me forward through passages that were once as familiar as my own face and were now as foreign as a new world. Over rubble and debris and, oh dear Heaven, was that a body? God help them. I pushed on, moving forward blindly. Past me grey shapes moved screaming about a murderer. I stopped and started after them. No, no! But they were running back into the flames, I couldn't follow. Not if I wanted to live. I allowed a brief flicker of thought about how nice it must be to just lay down and give up and be past all such concerns as living, but survival took over. Enough of that nonsense, it said, I did want to live. I desperately wanted to live! Tears were coming back, tears of frustration, and fear, and awful, wretched anger at the betrayal that had brought down this great Opera House and all within it. Damn. Damn! A flash of memory came unbidden: the snow, cool and fresh against my cheek. I had followed him up to the roof and watched unseen as he watched others unseen. Almost, almost I had gone to him when I heard his cries, until his cries turned to rage and I shrank away afraid the rage would be turned against me. Instead it had been turned against this entire great institution.

With a frustrated croak, I turned back, hauled up my skirts and retraced my steps, away from the fire, away from the vigilantes, away from all that futile longing. Damn! I moved, one hand against the wall for the air was getting perilously thin here and I was beginning to feel quite dizzy, down towards what I thought was the back of the Opera House by the stables. Another thirty feet and I stumbled against someone staggering in the hallway; a young woman, younger than myself, a ballerina, disoriented and blind. She was going down, she would not get out on her own, I knew. I could not just leave her. I grabbed her under her arms, screamed at her to get up, get up, damn you! And stumbled forward, dragging her along. Here at last was something I recognized; the door to the kitchens, far away from the blazing center of the fire. Maybe there would be an escape through there.

I pushed open the door, and slid in, pushing the young dancer ahead of me. There was smoke, how could there not be, but it was not as heavy here and I was able to stand mostly upright and see through the haze. The room was empty.

There, across the great wooden table, the door to the back courtyard and middens and from there, the street. How could there be no one else here? Or maybe the kitchen help had all fled already.

We went. Out into the courtyard, the grey cobbles reflecting the rust colored hell that was the burning of the Opera Garnier, and now I could at last hear other sounds; the screaming horses in the stables, the shouts of grooms, trying to lead the panicked beasts out and away, alarm bells, shouting crowds. How many had died? How many would still? How many friends would I never see again?

The dancer, enough air finally getting into her body to help her regain her senses, pulled away from me and without any notice of me, began to run. I ran too, but away from her. I kept running...past the stables, past the brigades, past the onlookers. I ran and ran and in my mind was one thought: did he yet live?

One

Paris, France: 1882

All was deathly still. I'd never seen the Opera House so quiet and empty. It was eerie enough to send a shiver through me, as though it existed in a world separate from the rest of Paris. A couple of carriages stood outside the soot darkened Grand Entrance, their drivers and horses dozing in the sun, so someone must be inside. Inspectors, perhaps? Maybe Messieurs Moncharmin and Richard, if they'd survived. I hadn't heard, and I'd not thought to ask. I hadn't heard much at all actually. The denizens of the Opera Garnier had been flung as far as the ashes still drifting idly down from the rooftops with any stray breeze. I'd seen a very few of the other seamstresses I'd known. I knew the great Soprano, Carlotta had sadly perished from the smoke, and I was glad to hear that my costume mistress, Mde. Odelle, had gotten out. She had ever been kind to me, though my stitches were not as good as they should be, I knew, and it was a joy to see my friends alive and well. But the one name I wanted to hear about, the one fate I so desperately needed to know, was still unknown. No one seemed to know the fate of the Opera Ghost. I wondered if anyone realized the fire had been his doing, but then, not many really realized he was anything more than a legend. I knew though. His world was our shared secret, though he was unaware he shared it with me. It had been a month since the explosions and fire that had turned the Opera House into this desolate wreck. I could no longer stand the mystery.

And so I found myself huddled here by the wall, watching, trying to plan which entrance I would use, knowing I needed to be circumspect. I would not be allowed in if anyone saw me. The building was deemed unsafe, and the scene of an active investigation into the cause of the fire. With the exceptions of the managers (or their replacements, perhaps, and only when escorted by the Gendarmerie), no one of us had been allowed in, not to try to collect any belongings that may have survived the fire, not to look for the missing, not for any purpose.

But not everyone knew the Opera House the way I did. I had taken to wandering the halls and passages almost the day I'd arrived, at age thirteen, and had never stopped. The face the Opera House put on was not the only one it possessed. There were passages behind most of the rooms. I supposed they were originally intended for servants and night refuse men to pass unseen and avoid insulting the refined noses of the Prima Donnas and Patrons and other dignitaries staying as guests. But they had been long abandoned, and I don't know that very many even knew they existed any longer. These were just one of the secrets belonging to this great building. I flatter myself to think I knew of most of them by the year I turned fifteen.

This day, as I waited by the wall for my chance, I was glad of my knowledge of my *Opera Secret*. It would get me into the building, I knew, and to where I needed to go without being seen. The question was which way in should I choose? Which was most hidden, and which posed the least risk of falling atop me as I scrambled in? Would it be the door under the front steps? No, too public. I couldn't make it in through the kitchen again, I knew that. It was much too exposed. No...just there...the left side of the building. There was an opening into a passage behind the stage for easy access during performances. It was partly hidden anyway from the view of the drive, and now it was hidden entirely behind stacks of refuse, but still accessible. And there was another smaller door just down the corridor once inside that would get me back behind the main rooms and walls. I could explore from there. That would be it then.

Trying to appear as just another curious passerby I idled my way around the side of the building towards the entrance I'd chosen. No one gave me even the slightest notice. Now that the moment had arrived to actually go back inside my stomach rolled over and I pressed my fist to it to quiet it. People had died here, people I had known. I had lived here and would never live here again. It was much to think about, but now was not the time, I told myself. If I stood here much longer someone was bound to notice me. Looking around one last time to be sure everything was clear, I made the fast dart from the street, turned the handle -thankfully it had not been locked- and opening the door only as far as needful, I slipped inside.

What I did not know then was that I had indeed been noticed and that mistake would change everything.

Pressing my skirts as close to the wall as possible, though why I thought that might hide me if someone was to be in the hall I really couldn't say, I checked up and down the corridor. No one. The air was still vaguely hazy and the smell of roasted fabric, wood and flesh was strong. I gagged, swallowing bile, realizing that some of the smell most likely was all that was left of people I had known. Tears stung my eyes, but I pinched my nose and resolutely took the few steps to the panel in the wall that I knew would open and allow me into the back halls of the Opera House.

When the panel clicked closed behind me I turned and, letting my eyes adjust to the dimness, got my bearings. The black soot changed the way it all looked and it no longer felt like my familiar old building, but some strange new continent. The absurd thought of my being a brave explorer on a daring expedition crossed my mind and I grinned idiotically at the picture this presented. Little me, with my snub nose and unruly hair in a many times too big metal helmet and military uniform like those I'd seen in the costume department, trudging through muggy jungles full of exotic birds and overgrown flowers. I snorted quietly to rid myself of the image. It somehow felt sacrilegious to laugh in here right now. Best concentrate on the job at hand.

Yes, I knew where I was in reference to the other hidden passages. To go to the right would lead me under the stage and from there to other parts of the main theatre building. To go to the left, however, would eventually take me round and then down to where the cellars lay. That was where I must go. The soot came off onto my hands when I touched the walls, and there were portions where those walls were collapsed and the inner passages were partly revealed, but those were few and quickly passed. As I moved farther and farther away from the front rooms where the explosions had happened and the fire had started, the damage gradually grew less and in a few turns the hidden corridors became hidden once again. There were spiders here and rats, but I'd long grown accustomed to them and was not afraid. I was surprised to see them so soon after the fire, I'd have thought they'd have long fled, but here they still were. Perhaps they had simply returned. Opportunists that they were, I am sure they found much to benefit from in this ruined shell. I moved, ducking under the trailing vines of long abandoned webs and stepping over piles of ancient play bills left in heaps and other refuse of a long gone age of the theatre.

The heavy metal grilled gate that sealed the cellars off from the main floors of the theatre was rusty and it took several seconds of my pushing against it to get it to move, but once it did I did not find it difficult going to get it open wide enough for me to squeeze in sideways. I pulled it back shut behind me. If someone were to happen to come down here I did not want them wondering at an open gate. I followed the dark stone steps down, down and farther down till they opened into a more lighted rotunda hung with dusty and faded tapestries that led yet farther down. I held the bannister and went down slowly, suspecting there were traps and tricks on the steps here that could easily lure me into an early grave.

At the bottom of the rotunda there was a choice before me: the cobbled corridor that led to the underground lake? Or the carved stone tunnel that led somewhere I had not explored yet? I had no way to cross the lake or travel the canals and to get wet wading them would lead to questions once I was back above ground that I could not answer. My decision made, I veered right and followed the low tunnels. They were very, very dark and the basques of lions and beasts were silent company as I made my way through them. I turned and double backed and retraced my steps a dozen times trying to get somewhere. What little light came in was just enough to allow me to see the turns and memorize my way back out. But the floor was steady and smooth, and the height consistent. I did not feel afraid. Not of my route. I was more worried about what I would find -or not find- at the end of my journey.

I found out a moment later. The corridor widened abruptly and opened into a windowless chamber built into the stone and set in a series of small rooms leading to one another. To the left were the edges of the underground lake, and in front of me was a chamber filled with the most incredible items and all in a state of supreme chaos. I don't know quite what I was expecting but this was not it. There was a carved bed shaped like a coffin with hangings of the finest black lace. These were mostly tossed to the ground and torn. There was an organ, covered in dust, tables of papers with diagrams and drawings and sketches, half of them strewed about the floor and covered with footprints or torn or both. Crumpled pages of musical scores, mirrors cracked and shattered glass everywhere. Candles that had burned to nothing, their wax pooled on the rock below and caking the red velvet curtains that were half pulled down. There was a dress form with a life like wax head attached overturned and lying at the very edge of the lake. It was damp and the hair of the manikin was trailing in the water, floating like river weed. It was not a little spooky. I turned away from it and moved throughout the chamber.

I had found what I was looking for. This then, was where he had lived. Could he live here still? It seemed deserted, for no one had done anything to right the chaos and destruction. Did this mean he no longer lived? Or that he had merely fled and not returned? Or was there another answer altogether? I stood a chair upright and sat upon it, pondering what to do next. I really had not thought what I'd do once I'd achieved my destination. So now what? I picked up a loose sketch from the floor and turned it over and over in my hands. It was of course of her, Christine Daae, the young diva who had spurned his love for that of the nobleman, the Viscomte De Chagny. I stared at the sketch, flattening the crumpled edges smooth against my thighs. She was very beautiful, with a sweetness of face and softness of figure that certainly I could never hope to achieve. It was no wonder he had loved her, no wonder the Viscomte had as well. What would have happened had not the Viscomte come to the Opera House when he had and turned her head? But he had, and The

Phantom's rage at the betrayal had quite destroyed everything.

A deep breath and I'd decided I was not ready to leave. I'd do what any woman in this place with nothing else planned would do: I'd tidy up.

I stood, tucked my skirts up into my belt a bit and looked around. Where to start? Well, right here I supposed, and I stooped to start gathering papers off the floor. I went about, gathering up papers, stacking them neatly on tables and desks, flattening the crumpled ones first, and setting heavy books down on the stacks to keep them in place and help to smooth the wrinkles out as well. I righted candelabras, and made a small pile of trash in a corner near the passage I'd entered the room from. I'd take what I could today and come back for the rest another time.

I was on my knees in front of a partly shattered full length mirror carefully brushing shards into a pile with a wadded up bit of torn fabric when I felt the hairs on the back of my neck stand straight up and an ice cold sensation as of a thousand insect legs traveled up my spine. My legs instantly turned to jelly and my stomach clenched. I lifted my head to the mirror. There was my reflection, gone ghostly pale, and behind it was The Phantom, no more than an arm's length from me.

I gasped and spun and shrank back against the mirror utterly unable to speak. My heart raced and spots danced before my eyes. I don't think I breathed. We stared at each other. Or rather, I stared, he glowered. It might have been a minute but it, of course, felt like forever that we remained there, frozen. It was long enough for my heart to slow and my breathing to resume and for me to regain some of my composure.

"Who are you?" he finally demanded. His voice was low and quiet, so very quiet. He hadn't moved.

"I-" My voice broke. I cleared it and tried again, "My name is Sophie."

Still he just stood there. I shifted, my knees were starting to hurt and I could feel the pressure of the broken mirror frame behind my hip.

"I was part of the-" I started in an attempt to fill the awful silence when he abruptly leapt forward and reached down, grabbing my arm roughly and hauling me to my feet.

I made a startled squeak of protest and then he leaned right down inches from my face and snarled, "What are you doing here, you trespassing little vermin?"

I could feel his breath against my cheeks, see the planes of his face on the side uncovered, the stubble of a beard not recently shaved, see the smoothness of the mask he wore, smell his scent of wax and sweat and wine and ink and something undeniably, overpoweringly male. My senses were completely alert, and a flush was spreading from my belly down my legs and up across my face. I was utterly aware of how vulnerable I was...and how female. But I was also, to my incredibly detached surprise, absolutely unafraid. He'd startled me, but I was not frightened.

And this absurd realization is what enabled me to do what I did next.

I leaned right back at him, steeled my voice and said firmly, "Stop that."

It was his turn to be startled. He dropped my arm and stepped back a bit. We stood there staring at one another again for another minute. Then I said, "I am not afraid of you."

He said simply, "Then you are a fool."

I didn't answer and we continued to stand there until I broke his gaze, knelt back down and resumed gingerly brushing the shards of broken glass again into the pile I'd begun. Half of them had been disturbed and knocked aside when he'd grabbed me. He just stood watching me. My nerves had had quite enough and I started to babble.

"I'll just tidy this up a little. Really, it's shameful, the mess. I can't stay much longer. I'll come back tomorrow or the next day with a broom perhaps. All right then, well, I'd best be going, they'll be missing me..." And I gathered a small armful of debris I'd stacked by the entrance to the passages and turned abruptly and left him.

I managed to get most of the way back through the stone corridors to the rotunda before my legs gave way and I slid against the wall to the cold dirty floor. I sat in a collapsed heap, with tears leaking from my eyes and sliding down my cheeks, my heart racing, my muscles as weak as newborn chicks. The fear that he was right behind me and would come upon me at any moment was strong and bitter in my stomach. I felt I might vomit from it and turned my head aside just in time not to splatter my shoes and skirts. Just under all this was an enormous sense of triumph and pride. He was alive, alive! And I had faced him. The exhilaration singing in my breast, I gathered myself, stood shakily, took up my small burden of trash once more and retraced my steps back out of the Opera House.

Two

I stepped out of the Opera House into the chilled air, rubbed goosebumps from my arms as my skin protested the extra cold, and took a step towards the street. Round the corner of the refuse pile stepped a man. I stopped dead. Medium height and build with a shock of dark hair slicked back, a strong jaw that did not hide a shadow of what must be a very full beard against olive skin, and surprisingly rich brown eyes, he was very handsome and quite sure of his attraction to women. He smiled, but I noticed the smile was not quite reflected in his eyes. I instantly did not trust him.

"Bon jour, Mademoiselle," he said. "I am Inspector Bruyere."

"Monsieur," I nodded at him and made to move away.

"Wait, Mademoiselle."

I stopped, very much aware of the pile in my arms, scraps of torn paper and sticks from broken furniture loosely wrapped in some of the discarded fabric to hold it all together.

"You are aware no one is allowed inside the Opera House at this time, are you not?" he asked.

I looked boldly at him and lied, and knew that he knew I was lying. "Oh? No, I did not. I wished to retrieve some belongings." I gestured at my burden. He looked and his eyebrows lifted. I kept my gaze on him steady and said, "I must go, my employers are expecting me." I walked away. Inanely I thought how cold my nose felt.

Behind me, the Inspector said, "Mademoiselle, you were in there a very long time to retrieve so few 'belongings'. I do not wish to see you here again, is that clear?"

I did not look back and I did not answer. I just kept walking, silently encouraging my quavering knees not to give way beneath me.

As I'd promised I went back the next day, Inspector be damned. I did not dare use the same way in this time for fear of once again being seen so I scouted carefully for an acceptable alternate before settling on one that involved crawling through a hedge, dragging my broom behind me. It worked however and this time I was absolutely certain no one had seen me.

I made my way back down the hallways, to the cellars and rotunda, and down the stone passageway. Once again, the chamber was empty upon my arrival. This time I knew what I was going to do once there, so I leant my broom against the bed and resumed cleaning up. I don't know why I'd settled on this chore as a necessary one, only that it felt wrong somehow to leave it as it was. If he was still staying there, it was inhuman and tragic for him to stay in this chaos. If he wasn't, then it was too much evidence of the recent sorrow. I could not fix the Opera House, but I could right this one small corner of it.

I spent about three quarters of an hour fussing here and there, and sweeping since I knew I'd need to return the broom. I dawdled hopefully as long as I could, but in the end, he never showed and I had to go. I would be somewhat late as it was and I dared not lose this position because the alternative was one I could not even contemplate. I consoled myself in the knowledge that there was much more to do and I would have to return for that.

I was unable to return to the Opera House the next day, but upon the following I did. The heavy velvet curtains made my arms ache as I took them down, standing on top of a low table I slid around the room to do so, and in the end I could only remove most of them, not all, and none of the black lace ones. I stacked them on one of the tables neatly folded, leaving a damaged pair by the Chamber entrance to take with me. Standing and surveying the room, my eyes went again to the manikin lying on its side near the water's edge. My stomach knotted when I looked at it, lying there as though drowned. It was a symbol of all that had gone wrong, and I did not want to touch it.

"This won't do," I muttered and moved to the water. I stood staring down at it, the fabric of the torso water stained and beginning to mildew, the face turned to the water, the hair still floating.

"Leave it."

His voice came from my right. I turned to see him standing near the tallest of the mirrors, the one that had suffered the most damage and was now mostly just a frame. "Leave it," he repeated.

"It can't stay like this. It's getting ruined," I nearly whispered. My heart raced.

"What does that matter? It's a perfect fate for it." He took a few steps further towards me. Waving a hand vaguely towards the manikin he mumbled, "It's all in ruin."

I watched as he came towards me. He was all in black, his shirt open at the throat and no ascot or four-in-hand. It occurred to me in some removed corner of my brain that he looked to be in mourning. My eyes strayed to his arm unconsciously, half expecting to see a black armband there. But he was cleanly shaved and his hair was in place and his mask straight. He must be taking some pains. What for, I wondered? Habit, perhaps?

"You keep coming here. Why? How did you find this place?" He asked, truly looking at me for the first time since he'd spoken.

My mouth felt of cotton, and my voice was quiet as I answered, "You are not the only one who knows the Opera House's secrets. I dared not come this far before, but it was not hard to find knowing what I know."

His eyes went dark and I blanched and whispered, "Please." I still do not know precisely what it was I was pleading for.

"And what, exactly, is that, pray tell?" he hissed.

I didn't answer right away, thinking of what to tell him. How to explain that discovering the secret door in the sewing room had opened up an entire new world to a lonely fifteen year old. The wonder at the dusty grey corridors, their lamps cold and empty, the golden rotundas, and alcoves above ceilings, the mirrors and doors that led to a world of enchantment and peace and much needed solitude? How do you tell someone that you had been a silent witness to their own pain, and knew their own secrets?

He took the necessity for such explanations away from me then.

"You have no right to be here, meddling, scurrying about these caverns like a mouse in shadows. This is no place for you, child." His voice was harsh but not, I think, truly angry.

"I'm not a child." My voice, even to me, sounded defensive. I was no child. At twenty-two I was close to being an old maid actually and had long accepted that destiny for myself. It irked me to have someone bring up lost hopes by mis-categorizing me.

He looked at me again and took a moment before answering. "No, you are not, after all." His eyes strayed round the room, taking in the upright candelabrums, the swept floor, the tidied papers and then went again to the manikin in the green water. "That doesn't alter the fact that you should not be here."

"I don't mean to pry, I assure you. This was my home too, I miss it now it's gone. I just wanted to have somewhere to go..." I broke off, then finished with, "I thought perhaps you'd need a friend."

"I need no one."

"Oh, I can see that," I said wryly. "You are so clearly deliriously content all alone." Oh God, my tongue was going to get me into such trouble. It always did. I looked at my feet. The toes of my boots were getting wet from the gentle lapping of the cold water against the stone I stood on. My toes would get chilled. I stepped back.

He laughed. A genuine, honest laugh. Well, a chuckle really, but it was laughter from a most unexpected source. It took me completely by surprise so I looked up at him, and the un-hidden half of his face had altered and became shockingly charming and magnetic.

"You are a brave little thing." He said, "Why are you not afraid of me?"

"Because I know what a real monster looks like and where to find one, and it's not in someone's face." The acidic words had slipped out before I truly knew what I was saying. I almost gasped at my audacity, but stood steady, waiting to see what he would do.

A shadow passed over his countenance then and he bowed to me. "Wisely said, Little Mouse."

We stood looking at one another for a moment and it was in that moment that I felt the first hint of connection. Perhaps he did need a friend after all.

I knelt back down to the manikin and grabbed it by the throat, pulling it up with me as I stood. The Phantom said nothing, did nothing. I carried it across the rock and stood it out of the way near a wall.

"She is lovely and very sweet and her voice is like an angel," I said, "but she could not have survived a life with you. She is too gentle, surely you must know that."

He said nothing, just stood still as death.

"You nearly brought this entire building down and many innocent people were hurt. All for nothing."

"It was...unfortunate," he mumbled.

Knowing this to be as close to an acknowledgement of guilt and an apology as he was capable of, I nodded slightly to him, then went to the velvet hangings, picking up a pair of them. He watched me as I bundled them up and moved to the passage. I looked back at him over my shoulder, "I'll repair these and bring them back in a few days when I can get away again."

He nodded.

I left.

Behind me I thought I heard him whisper, "As you like, Little Mouse," but I could not be sure.

I moved down the Rue Auber and turned onto Rue Boudreau heading towards the home of my employer. On the night of the fire I had fled to my cousin, who worked for M. Gaudet as valet to his eldest son. Where else could I go? Henri and indeed the entire household had heard the alarms and could see the fire raging in the ninth *arrondissement*, and the staff had taken my wretched, soot covered and coughing self in for the night. Bathed and dressed in castoff clothing that ill-fitted but were clean I was presented the next morning to the Master and Mistress of the House.

"She has been gently raised, Monsieur, Madame, and is a fine seamstress. She would be a great benefit to your household," Henri enticed, cap in his hands in front of him. I stood quietly with my head down.

"Marcel," Mde. Gaudet had said to her husband, buttering a baguette, "we must needs do our best to show charity to those poor souls affected by the fire. She seems a good quiet girl, do let's help. Amelie was just telling me she is falling behind in the mending. This girl could be of great assistance to her. And in the scullery as well, perhaps."

She smiled kindly at me and I chanced a small smile of my own in return, then hid my face again.

And so I was given a bed in the servants' quarters. This was a tiny cell of a room, mostly a closet, but big enough for a small pallet on the floor and some few hooks on the wall. It was quiet and very warm and mine and I felt safe curled into my pallet at night. And it was near to Henri and that gave me great joy. My cousin was 8 years older and as a child I had worshiped him. When he left our family to work for the Gaudet's as a young man of 15, I had grieved madly. He was my one confidante and being close to him now was a great comfort.

Shifting my burden of curtains once again to my other hip, I turned the corner and my heart sank. Just there, lounging against the wall halfway up the block, hands in pockets and a cap pulled down low was a man. Armand. He was in his late 30s perhaps, stocky, with a sort of boyish face that had probably been charming as a young man but now merely made him seem pouty and disagreeable. He wore his blonde hair greasy and too long to be fashionable and he always seemed slightly unkempt. I was not sure from where in the neighborhood he came from, but I had seen him several times in the area. He always paid me just that much too much attention. I felt his eyes swing to me, and I made to cross the street. He pushed off from the wall and intercepted me.

"Allo, Mademoiselle, *Ca va*?" he said with a sly sort of charm.

I ignored him, put my burden between him and myself, and kept walking. He fell into step beside me. "Come now, Mademoiselle, I am only trying to be friendly. Why won't you talk to me, eh?"

He stepped in front of me, forcing me to halt. My heart froze. "Leave me alone," I managed to croak, and moved around him.

For a mercy he didn't follow, merely laughed as I hurried away. I felt tears from an ancient wound burn behind my eyelids and forced them away. In a few moments I was at the Gaudet's home and I went into the servants' entrance and up to my cabinet with relief.

Three

I t had taken me a few days to repair the curtains, but they were done and ready to hang and so I made my accustomed trek to the underground chamber. The Phantom was, as usual, not there when I arrived but there was a package neatly tied with brown paper and black ribbon laid purposefully atop the larger desk. There was a note sealed with red wax tucked into the ribbon. I cracked this and read,

"Little Mouse,

I noticed that you seem frequently chilled and lack a proper wrap against the cold. Take these, with my compliments.

Your Servant,
The Phantom"

I read and reread the missive. Then with trembling hands I untied the ribbon, set it aside and removed the brown paper. Within was a pair of soft woolen gloves in a color of green like the moss on the stones in The Tuilleries, delicately embroidered in a darker forest green. With these was a matching wrap, long enough to cover most of my thighs. They were quite simply beautiful, nicer than most anything I'd ever owned. I was so astounded I couldn't even react. I just stood there holding these to my face. They smelled of wool, and some musky cologne. A man's scent, not a woman's. Where did he get these things?

He knelt in the shallow alcove above the Chamber watching her as she discovered the gift he'd left for her and opened it. She appeared to like it. This was good. He was not accustomed to having to follow the niceties of polite society, but he thought a gift was an appropriate response to the efforts she had been putting in on his behalf, wanted or not, and really she did appear distressingly ill-equipped for the season's increasing chill.

She glanced up, searching the room, looking towards the passages and the lake, probably looking for his appearance. Would he show himself today? He thought. No, perhaps not. He honestly would not know what to say if she fawned over his gift. Maybe now she would take it and go and leave him in what tortured peace he could find. Is that what he truly wanted? Damn, he didn't honestly know what he wanted anymore. He only knew what he understood and that was not having visitors on a regular basis. How in God's name had she found these chambers in the first place?

She had put the gloves on and draped the shawl round her shoulders and was admiring them in what remained of a mirror. She turned this way and that, preening and he could not keep the edges of his mouth from turning upwards. He watched a little while longer, silently, as she put the gifts down neatly and sat at the desk doing something he could not quite see with her back to him blocking his view. She then proceeded to re-hang the curtains she had returned. When they were up, she bustled about choosing more curtains to take for repairs, and then with a last look around she wrapped herself back up in his gifts and left via the stone corridors.

He waited a few minutes, and worked his way down to his old rooms. It was almost returned to its former state. Almost. But it would never be home to him again, that was certain. Her efforts were largely wasted. Still, they were a kind gesture and had prompted his gesture in return. A few minutes scouting shop windows at night, then half an hour waiting in shadows at dusk for the boy he'd paid to purchase the gift for him and it was done. Far less time than she had spent, but he hoped a worthy payment for her work. He moved to the desk and saw that she had also taken the note with her, and the ribbon he had wrapped the package in, but left the brown paper. On it, she had written something. Ah yes, indeed, the ink and quill were there once more; retrieved during one of her cleaning sprees from the floor where he'd left them lie.

He took the paper, folded it carefully, and slipped it inside his shirt. Then he left the room behind.

"Oo la la...Sophie has a suitor!"

"Amelie!" I gasped. "Do not say such things."

"Where did you get such a beautiful wrap then, and those gloves, eh?" She teased. The other servants in the kitchen laughed with her.

"Come now, Sophie, tell us, who is your young man?" they badgered. "Perhaps you have finally taken to Armand, eh? He has been following you for weeks!"

"There is no one, truly, no one. Armand, no! I'd rather die. They were just...they were..." Unable to think of a decent explanation, I bolted from the room up to the safety of my cabinet, their good natured laughter following me up the back stairs.

My cousin joined me there soon after. I had tucked the curtains under my blanket, and slipped the gloves and wrap further down under the pallet itself. I was playing with the black ribbon, wondering if it would hold back my heavy mane of hair that was all colors and no color at all, brown, auburn and blond and so straight it defied any attempt at the curls of today's fashions. Perhaps to tie a braid? Mayhap it would hold then.

Henri took the ribbon from my hands and turned me with my back to him. He sat beside me on my pallet and pulled the front sections of my hair away from my face deftly. Joining them together in the back, he wrapped the ribbon around these sections several times then tied it into a bow, letting the ends hang. It was a young style. I should be too old for it, but left it nevertheless.

I turned to face him.

"It is not the height of fashion, but it will have to do as I am only used to dressing a man's hair and the current feminine styles are beyond me," he said. "So, Cousin is it true? Is there a man?" he asked kindly.

I shook my head. "Not really, Henri. I promise you." But there was flush rising to my cheeks and Henri saw it.

"Cousin, you can confide in me."

"I do know, but Henri..." I broke off. "It is nothing. There is a person I have been visiting, someone all alone. He gave the gifts to me. That is all, truly. It is nothing."

"Who is this person, does he need assistance? Is he feeble in some way? I should, perhaps, accompany you on your visits?"

"No, Henri!" The variety of disastrous results that could occur should I dare to bring anyone else down below the Opera House whirled through my mind like a maelstrom and I reacted rather more strongly than I intended.

Henri had moved back sharply at my wail, and his eyebrows had drawn together. He was about to speak again but I put a hand to his chest to stop him, "Henri, I am sorry, I did not mean to speak so. It's just very complicated. There are reasons I must go alone, but I am not putting myself into any danger." I hoped my eyes did not show the doubt I felt at that last statement. It was at best only half true. "Please just trust me. I will be fine."

Henri regarded me, then sighed and smiled. "Since you were first old enough to toddle about you have followed me like a puppy. My mother bade me watch you always lest you fell down and bumped your behind and cried. For more than 20 years I have done so. It is a difficult habit to break now, but you are no longer a puppy, are you?"

I shook my head.

"Well then Cousin, I will not hover so, but if you tumble and hurt your backside, I will merely say I told you so *comprenez-vous*?"

"Thank you, Henri." I reached forward and hugged him tight. He held me in return for a moment then released me and stood.

"Come, there is tea in the kitchens." he invited. I stood, shut the door to my cabinet and followed him down to tea.

Four

It seemed I was destined for a day of bad fortune the next time I headed out for the Opera House. I had no sooner left the Gaudet home when I spotted the sly Armand lurking on the corner with two companions, just as disheveled as he was, and all sharing a hand rolled cigarette. Tapping his friends' shoulders as I came down the steps he started towards me. I turned on my heel and headed back into the house. Henri was not at home, as he was waiting upon his gentleman, and so I stayed within the house until I could see Armand had given up and left the street. I quickly hurried down the street in the other direction, and taking the long way, resumed my journey to the Opera House.

Again I was to be thwarted, for as I neared the Opera, I saw figures standing on the steps, and recognized one of these as Inspector Bruyere, the same Inspector who had caught me emerging from the side door my first day visiting The Phantom. My stomach sinking, I dropped my head and kept walking, but from the corner of my eye saw him glance up and catch sight of me. He watched me as I went past. I dared not return his gaze, just kept my head low and continued on, trying to appear for all the world as if I were just out and about my normal business.

After that I feared to attempt a foray into the Opera House, and besides, too much time of my short break from employment had already past. So I gave up for the day and taking a circuitous route to avoid Armand should he have reappeared, headed back to the home of my employers.

I tried again the next day and luck was with me this time. No Armand and no one outside the Opera House. To be safe, I chose again yet another secret way inside the building, this time a low window that was mullioned and partly hidden by a column. It pushed up from the bottom, and I clambered inside. Really, it was quite a wonder my skirts were not completely ruined with all this scrambling on my knees. But they were happily surviving, dirty, but very little the worse for wear otherwise.

I made my way to The Phantom's Chamber, and for the first time he was there when I arrived. I don't think he'd been waiting just for me, as he was involved in something, but it gave me a start to see him when I'd grown used to having him appear after my arrival.

"Good day, Monsieur." I managed.

He did not look up, but he nodded. "You are making use of the gifts I left for you, I see."

I stroked the soft wool of the wrap with pleasure. "Yes, they are wonderful. Thank you." I made to take off my gloves and wrap, but he stood and motioned for me to stop.

"No, leave them on, you will need them. Come..." and taking me unceremoniously by the arm, he led me out of the chamber.

For a moment, I thought he was removing me from the Opera House as we started back the way I'd come in. I dared not say anything, my heart beating hard in my chest, but as we got to the bottom of the rotunda, he turned and went another direction.

"Where are we going?" I finally braved.

He stopped and gave me a look as though the fact I would not know had not even occurred to him. "To the roof." he said, not unkindly, and led on to another staircase, darker, steeper, and more direct, probably a maintenance stairway. "You can make it up these steps?"

I smiled a little wickedly and nodded, "I know these stairs actually." I lifted my skirts and moving out of his grasp, started up them quickly.

"Clever Little Mouse" I heard him murmur behind me as I moved upwards. We went up several floors and then he put a hand out to stop me. He gestured to a door. Opening it, he motioned me through. We had entered a room, dark and still smelling vaguely of smoke. A prop room. I stood just inside the entrance, my eyes adjusting to the dim light, even dimmer than that on the stairs.

The Phantom took a step past me and turned to me, beckoning with one hand. Behind him stood a rank of papier mache statues of Greek and Roman Gods, standing in a cluster, their naked white forms in stark relief against the black of the Phantom's trousers, shirt and waistcoat. I followed, as he moved serpentine-like past one then another in a winding labyrinth. Once past the statues, we moved through a mystical world of faux gilded furniture, painted mountains and balconies on canvas, garlands of paper flowers and wooden balconies lying on their sides.

My eyes were glued as though hypnotized to The Phantom's back lest I lose him in this enchanted Otherworld and be bound to wander forever. He turned once to be sure I still followed and the smooth white of his half mask stood out as the faux statues had in contrast to the black hair and startling blue/green eyes, turned a smoky silver grey in this hazy light. I was vaguely aware of the sound my boot heels made on the wooden floor, tiny hollow tappings, with each step. The Phantom made no sound as he drifted through the room, no sound at all and I began to wonder if maybe my assessment of him as merely a man was wrong and he was indeed some spectral ghost out of myth. But then he reached out to grasp my hand and help me over a low stack of wooden crates filled with platters and cups and I knew him to be a man again when the heat of his hand reached through the chill of my own skin.

We entered another door and climbed another short stair and stopped at yet another door. The Phantom opened this one and we stepped out onto a breezy rooftop terrace. It seemed the magic was not to have ended at the prop room, because in front of me was all of Paris, gloriously lit on fire with the pinks and peaches and indigos of a perfect sunset.

"Oh!" I breathed.

The Phantom's mouth turned up very slightly at this. He led me to a sheltered nook near a statue and we sat without speaking where we could gaze out over the rooftops before us.

It was a few moments before I remembered what I had brought with me. I dug into the pockets of my skirts and came up with two oranges; a treasure given me by Mde. Gaudet's daughter in exchange for repairing some tears in her riding habit that she'd thought un-mendable. I had hoarded them for days waiting for the opportunity to bring them here to share. I handed one silently to The Phantom now.

He took it, looked at it, then at me, "An orange?"

I smiled and began to peel my own. He murmured a thank you and followed suit. We sat in relatively companionable silence till our treats were peeled.

I took a bite of the fruit, savoring its sharp, sweet juice and after swallowing it, braved a question. "Why did you bring me up here?"

"I do get tired of wallowing in the dark occasionally. Besides, the sunset is always beautiful after a fire. There is enough ash still in the air to make this one worth viewing, yes?"

"Many people died in this fire though," I murmured. It needed to be said.

We lapsed back into silence and I studied his face as he looked out over the city and popped orange slices into his mouth. He was sitting to my right so I had a good view of the unmarked half of his face. A strong jaw, straight nose and heavy brow, dark hair slicked back over a smallish ear. His lashes were dark, over those aquamarine eyes, and his lips were full.

He was tall, and carried himself with a straight and proud bearing, none of the softness that burdened so many men once they were past their 30s. Without the damage to the right side of his face that pulled that side of his mouth up slightly when he spoke, he would have been considered, if not exactly beautiful, quite attractive. And there was a maleness to him that defied all expectations of what was considered beautiful and compelled one to look, even beyond the mask. It was a sense of barely constrained danger, a tension, like that I imagined you'd find in a wolf or other predator of the deepest forests. I had heard of a menagerie at Versailles, built by our late King, Louis XVI, and the beasts he had there. Lions and tigers and spotted cats called leopards. I imagined them pacing in cages, longing for freedom, feral and dangerous and always ready to pounce, and thought they were probably very like The Phantom. I found myself unable to look away, though I blushed with the realization of the thoughts that went through my mind. I was long past such speculation, and certainly had no business contemplating it here. With this man of all men.

I blinked to rid my head of such foolishness and realized he had finished his orange and was looking back at me. His gaze dropped briefly to my own treat and I realized I'd stopped eating with several slices still left.

"Oh, here, are you still hungry? I am not anymore, you can have mine!" I quickly pulled away a slice and leant forward and without thinking reached it towards his mouth.

His eyes flew to mine and his lips parted slightly. He stared at me, and I stared back, neither of us moving. I was frozen, those eyes holding me, then he broke the gaze by shifting his eyes downwards to the orange slice and opening his mouth slowly wide enough to accept it. I gently slid the slice between his lips, and sat back on my hands, feeling the heat scorching my cheeks.

The rest of the orange sat in my lap, cradled in my skirts, and for some reason I sat looking at it as though it was positively the most fascinating thing I'd ever seen.

After a moment, The Phantom said, "May I?" and I looked up to see him gesturing to the remaining few slices in my lap. I handed them to him and he ate them.

"If I could undo it, I would," he said. "The fire, I would undo it. I have had a...interesting relationship with fire. It seemed the thing to do at the time."

I could think of nothing to say to such a speech. I merely nodded.

We sat there watching the very last of the sun drop below the roof line and as it did I was shaken back to reality. "Oh my goodness, I am dreadfully late! I must go!"

I scooped up the orange peels and stuffed them into my skirt pockets. The Phantom joined me and with his hand on my arm we made our way back down the small staircase, through the maze of the prop room, and back to the staircase by the cellars. I stopped there and pulled away.

"It's shorter if I go from here," I said.

He nodded and said, "Farewell then, Little Mouse."

I wanted to ask if I should come again, suddenly wanting very badly to hear him say yes, but I was still afraid the answer would be the exact opposite, so I said nothing, just turned and moved away. When I looked back, The Phantom had disappeared.

Once again I walked up Rue Auber, my mind full of a whirl of thoughts and emotions I could not quite fathom and was not sure what to do with. I was so distracted that it was a second before I realized someone had fallen into step beside me. I turned my head to see Inspector Bruyere walking beside me, not looking at me. My blood turned to ice, and I felt my face turn pale.

"Out for a late stroll, Mademoiselle?"

Wordless, I nodded.

"It is a wonder we keep running into one another, is it not? Funny, that we should haunt this same part of Paris, no?"

He held a largish bunch of papers rolled tightly in one hand and swung these up, arms akimbo in assumed bafflement.

"I work very nearby, Monsieur." I managed in almost a whisper.

"Hmm? What was that? I could not hear you, Mademoiselle," he stated blandly.

I swallowed and lifted my head a bit. "My employer's home is not far from here, and I live within his house. It is natural I should be in the neighborhood, do you not think? I rather suspect the question is why you are always here?" There went my treacherous mouth again. Curse it all to hell.

"Oh there you are mistaken! It is my job to be here in fact!" he said, a look of obvious false insouciance on his face. "I am investigating the fire at the Opera House. And the murders there, of course." this last said with a veiled hint of malice. "It is my belief that the madman responsible is still at large, Mademoiselle, and that he had and still has, perhaps, help."

"Why would you think that?" I asked, fear a frozen brick in my belly.

"It is very clear! No body was ever found, so the chances are he is both alive and still hiding in the Opera House, or he has fled. For either he would need help, do you not think?"

And once again, my treasonous mouth betrayed me for I blurted, "I think you are underestimating The Phantom very badly! I think he needs no help at all."

I realized we had stopped walking and were facing one another like opponents on a chess board. I held my breath, waiting for his response.

At last he said, sotto voce, "You seem to know better than I, Mademoiselle." Then he breathed very deeply and took hold of my arm. "Come, I will escort you to your employers. It does not do for you to be out unaccompanied with it getting so dark. Not with this madman still at large, and so very...capable, no?"

I walked beside him, trying to be casual and all the while feeling I might scream. I had to get back to the Opera House! I had to. I could not. There was no way I could risk it right now, even if no one was expecting me back to work, which they most certainly were. It would do no good for me to lose my employment or I'd be cast out and have to return to the home of my childhood and that I could not, must not, ever do! No, I must bide my time and wait.

One part of my frantic mind registered the sight of Armand scurrying off at the sight of the two of us and I was considering just how the worst of circumstances could deliver small mercies, when we arrived at the gate of the Gaudets' home.

I shrugged off the hand still holding my arm loosely and turned to the inspector. "This is it. You are free of your duty to see me safely home, Inspector. Thank you for your most...kind attentions."

The Inspector bowed low to me and as he did so, he took a much exaggerated deep breath. As he stood he said, "You smell of oranges, mademoiselle. I hope you enjoyed the treat of them."

I did not know what to say and so said nothing.

He took a few steps away, then turned to me and with his eyes brows pinched together he nodded in my direction and said, "You should take a care for your clothing, Mademoiselle. That is too fine a shawl to be covered so in dust."

Then he turned and headed down the walk. I stood until he was long gone. He could not watch me forever, this very determined Inspector, this man who thought he knew things, this utter pest!

He was making his way back to his lair, his mind turning and re-turning over the events of the day -the orange!- when he heard a noise coming from somewhere no noise should be coming from. He stopped, his senses on alert, and listened. It was certainly not the girl. She'd have no reason to be in that part of the Opera House, she'd gone long since. And it was certainly too late in the day for anyone on legitimate business here to be about.

With an abrupt change of direction he headed back the way he'd come till he reached a crossing. There he went left and worked his way along the corridor until he came to a well-like shaft that led up through several floors of the Opera House. He stopped and listened, intent. He knew where the sounds were originating. He headed that direction, keeping to the secret passages and tunnels that were his particular domain. Once on the second floor of the Opera House, he followed a dusty grey corridor till he reached what appeared to be a dead end. He pressed one hand to the wall towards the left side and that portion of the dead end swung inwards silently. He let himself into the room it opened into: one of the dressing rooms, everything silent and slightly ashy. He moved through it and into the corridor beyond. Down to the end and he entered another secret hallway and moved to where he knew the noises were coming from. A tiny panel in the wall slid open at his touch and he peered through and saw the maker of the unwelcome sounds.

He recognized the man, an Inspector. He had been here a few different times since the night of the great fire, picking through rubble and rubbish, taking bits and pieces away with him, talking to those vigilantes who had managed to find his original chambers that night, generally making a nuisance of himself, but till now a harmless nuisance as far as The Phantom was concerned.

Yet here he was poking in places he should not be, had no reason to be. There was nothing here to do with the fire. The only reason he could be here is if he was looking for The Phantom himself. In the Inspector's hands was a stack of wide papers, opened but with its edges curled, as though they'd been rolled before he arrived. Architectural drawings, clearly of the Opera House. This did not bode well.

The Inspector moved out of the room casually, and moved to another. He poked and prodded, and as the room grew darker, he took up a lamp and lit it with a phosphorus match from his pocket. He continued throughout the Opera House, looking through each room he came to as though for a hidden treasure. The Phantom followed, out of sight, and silent as his name implied. Following the plans in his hands, the Inspector gradually made his way to the main stairway up to the roofs. He tried the door but it didn't move. He leaned against it heavily. It would not budge, it was well locked. Putting the drawings down, he stepped back a few steps, then lifted his foot and kicked as hard as he could at the door. The lock snapped and the door opened with a solid smack against the wall behind it.

The Phantom frowned...such unnecessary destruction! He moved out onto the roof to one of his favorite vantage points, hidden from view but where he could see and hear everything.

The Inspector wandered about the roof terrace, never even glancing at the wonder of Paris spread out before him, its lights glowing golden in the early evening dark. The Phantom watched him running his hands along statues, and windows and gables. Watched as he knelt by the place where Sophie and The Phantom had sat and ate oranges while the sun set, and picked up one small lonely piece of orange peel that had been left behind. The Inspector turned this over and over in his fingers, bringing it up to his nose to breathe in the scent. With a look at last out across the rooftops, he slipped the piece of peel into a pocket and turned to go.

The Phantom followed him back down and watched as he finally left the Opera House, leaving The Phantom to contemplate this new development. Perhaps it was time to reassess his opinion of the amount of trouble this Inspector could cause?

The following day passed dreadfully slowly as I flew through my work, waiting for near dark before attempting to get to the Opera House. I was nervous and jumped at every shadow and sound as I moved along the streets and boulevards towards the dark shell of the magnificent building. I slipped into the Opera House using the same entrance through the bushes I'd been using before. Perhaps my use of the window is what had alerted the Inspector of my presence? I wasn't sure but was not going to take any chances.

I hurried down to the cellars softly calling his name, the name I'd not dared use before, "Eric? Eric, can you hear me? Please, be there."

He must have heard me, because he stepped out of the shadows right before I entered his lair and put a hand on my arm, startling me into silence.

He put his hands on both my arms and turned me to face him, saying, "I am here."

"There's a man, an Inspector, he's been following me." I started.

"Yes, I know. Come with me," he said.

He pulled me behind him to another nearby cavern, empty of anything but a small, narrow boat with a tall ornamental prow and a long oar, pulled partly up onto the rock. He helped me down to the water and into the vessel, then pushed it off the rock and stepped in as it moved away from shore. He stood at the back and rowed us out of the bay the cavern made and into the main part of the underground lake. He was wearing a white shirt this time, open at the throat, and no coat and I could see the muscles of his chest and arms and shoulders working as he pushed against the water. He rowed in silence and I sat in the front of the boat looking around at the lake. I had never been to the center of it before, of course, and it was lovely in its way. It smelled of damp and cold, and slightly fishy and there was a bare hint of something rotting or fermented, but it was still and green and all around were the walls of the caverns which had created it, brown and gold and rust and grey, worn smooth by years beyond counting of water. There were strange formations hanging from the ceilings, like icicles of stone, and areas in the walls where everything glinted and shone as of a million diamonds. The torch at the end of the prow glinted off these in facets of sparkling golden light.

"It's like a fairy story in here," I said into the hush.

"Is it?" he answered.

"Yes. Like a magic story where the Princess finds herself in some magical world with the Handsome Prince on the most extraordinary adventures."

"Hardly a handsome prince," he said flatly.

"Oh, I wouldn't say that," I answered, enchanted beyond belief at the magical lake and this magical boat taking me across it, "You're quite pleasant when you're not scowling like some Beast."

"And you're very free with your words, aren't you?" he scowled, in perfect contrast to my previous statement.

"I'm dreadfully sorry. That was rude of me," I apologized. "I sometimes can't control my tongue."

"I have observed that, Little Mouse."

"It's true, though." I ventured, "What I said. At least, I believe it is."

"In that case, I shall endeavor to appear pleasant more often to appeal to your delicate sensibilities." He mocked and made me a little bow.

After a moment more I said, "The man, the Inspector I mentioned? His name is Bruyere. He has been following me, I think. "

"I know. I have seen him."

"You have?"

"Yes, last night. He was here sniffing around like a hound. He found one of your orange peels. And he has been here before."

I should have known The Phantom would have noticed him. He had always seen everything. Well, everything but me that is.

He continued, changing the subject, "You called me by my given name earlier. How did you come to know it? No one has called me that for a long time."

"I overheard it spoken of once, when I was hiding in a closet. I remembered it, that's all."

He didn't answer.

"Is it all right that I call you so?"

Still no answer. I turned back to the water. We were moving from the lake into the mouth of a canal. Bordered by fawn colored stone with an arched ceiling overhead, these canals were man-made, unlike the lake which was natural. I knew the canals, but had not traveled them, and did not know where they led. They were just water ways under the Opera House and Paris streets. Drainage, no doubt.

Eric- for I had decided to answer my own question and think of him thus- kept rowing silently, rhythmically. There were basques of lion heads set periodically along the wall. Eric's torch lit each one as we came upon it, throwing it into golden light and shadow. They baffled me as they seemed to be somewhat like fountains until I realized they were probably fonts for water to drain into the canals from the street above. Only we French would create such beauty in such a place, I mused.

Still he rowed us onwards. It was a few moments before I realized he was singing to himself, something quiet and half under his breath. It was not the first time I had heard him singing. He sang often, and I'd heard him many times as I crept along the halls. It was the first time he'd sung knowing I was in his presence, and it seemed a gift. His voice was smooth and mellow and I relaxed into the journey, as we traveled smoothly along the tranquil surface of the water towards some unknown destination.

It was some time before Eric maneuvered the little craft to a sort of mooring and helped me step out. We walked along a gangway of sorts for several yards before Eric stopped before a door. He pushed it open and we stepped out onto a ledge underneath one of the bridges spanning the great River Seine. He sat on this and then helped me to sit. We remained there, watching the great snaking river as it flowed past, hearing the noises from the street and bridge above, the voices of passersby, and hawkers selling their wares, the carriages on the bridge, horses clopping by.

"Yes, it is all right," Eric finally said.

"What is?" I asked.

"If you wish to call me by my Christian name. It is all right, Little Mouse."

I smiled at him. He lifted the corner of his lips in a small smile in return.

"Be wary of the Inspector, Little Mouse. He is not unintelligent," he said. "I have brought you away from my old chambers in order to avoid leaving any more tell-tale signs of your presence. It would be unfortunate for you to be associated with me."

I nodded in agreement, at once afraid and strangely reassured.

"Stay here. I have an errand I must see to. I will only be a few moments," he said.

I started to scramble to my feet, but he put a hand on my arm and shook his head. "Stay here."

I settled back onto my perch and watched while he nimbly jumped down to the quay and pushed back into the shadows under my ledge. I could see only the black shape of him but it was enough to see that he scanned the surrounding quay once before setting off briskly up the walkway, pulling his hood up over his head. In seconds he had disappeared from sight and I sat, waiting a little nervously and feeling somewhat foolish. What was this mysterious errand and why did he not wish me to see him at it? With nothing else to do I picked at some loose threads in my black skirts and counted cracks in the quay. I was up to forty-seven when he returned.

He swung himself up to the ledge, and motioned to the door. "We should return. I will leave you closer to the rotunda. You can find your way from there? "

I nodded and took the hand he offered me to help me stand.

Back once more to his little boat and again on the canals, silently drifting our way back to the familiar underground passages of the Opera House.

Five

enri saw me as I came home and he moved to join me as I made my way to the work room. I was working on some mending of tablecloths I very much wanted to finish before the end of the day. If I did, it would free up more of my afternoon tomorrow. I was humming as I picked up my mending and sewing basket and sat on the stool by the fire. He stood opposite me.

"If I did not know any better, Cousin, I'd say you are in love." He teased.

I looked up from my sewing, alarmed, "Don't be absurd, Henri, I am too old now for such girlish nonsense."

"Twenty-two is hardly old, Sophie, and matters of the heart know no age anyway. We are French; we are in love with love itself! Come now, look at you, you are singing, there is a flush to your cheeks I have not seen for donkey's years, and you can't stop smiling lately. If it is not love, then perhaps you have discovered an opium salon," he joked.

I laughed in spite of myself, "Of course not. You are imagining things. I am just myself; Sophie, the same as I ever was." But inside I wondered. Could that be what the pounding heart and shortness of breath whenever I was near the Opera House meant? My God, could I be falling in love with the Phantom of the Opera? Had I quite lost my mind?

Henri must have seen my thoughts mirrored on my face for he said kindly, "Sophie, I have been in love, I know what it looks like. Tell me."

I looked up at Henri, my first hero, my one true champion and the best friend of my life, and my eyes welled and I could not stop myself from saying, "I think you may be right, Henri, and it is the most inappropriate person!"

"I am listening, dear heart."

"He...he is...an invalid, of a sort. He cannot come out of his place of residence. So I travel to him. We just talk, or not talk sometimes. I just am there, to be a companion, but I think he has become a companion for me as well now."

"This is the same person you told me of before, yes? Is he old, is that why he cannot enter society?"

"No, no it is not like that. He is strong in body, and about your age, maybe a little older, but he is...scarred, rather badly. And the world has been a cruel place for him." An understatement certainly. The merest glance at his disfigurement had caused an entire world to turn from him, and the one woman he had loved to betray him. Was it any wonder his genius had turned to rage?

"Does he return your affection?"

I sat back, laying my sewing down in my lap and stared into the flames of the little fire in the hearth. "I honestly don't know. I can't think so. But he allows my presence, and this is not his usual habit. Truly, though, Henri, that can't matter. It is an entirely inappropriate match and completely impossible." I laughed briefly, not meaning it. "I have gotten very good at guarding my feelings and fortifying my heart. Have no fear of my having dashed hopes."

"I don't fear for your hopes, Cousin, I fear for your heart. I fear you have walled it up inside an impenetrable fortress where no one can hurt you ever again," he said quietly but boldly.

I stared, my fists pressed into my stomach. Henri did not ever bring up the ancient wound, the old terror, the torture of my childhood. Never. How could he? How did he dare? I wanted never to remember the feel of cold meaty hands, the smell of sour wine and rotten teeth, the weight pressing me down, down till I thought I would smother with it. And the pain of young flesh, bruised and torn. Tears stung my eyes and I stood. I shook my head and pressed my fists to my eyes, hoping to erase such thoughts with the pressure against my eyelids. I started to leave the room.

Henri reached out and took my shoulders in his hands. I shook him off. "Don't touch me, not now."

But he had succeeded in halting my exit from the room, and so he dropped his hands away.

I composed myself and after a moment asked, "Why? How do you dare speak of it?"

"I am sorry if I distressed you. You know I would not cause you pain for all the world. But I have watched you dismiss any potential suitor you have ever had. You don't even give me the chance to disapprove of him before you have done it for me!" he said with some humor and I could not stifle a small bitter laugh at this. He pulled a small irregularly shaped object from his pocket, about two or three inches long and smaller in width. He took my hand and placed the object face up in my palm. It was the rough, off white shell of some sea creature that had lived and died and left this piece of evidence of its existence behind. "Do you see, Sophie, how rough this side is, how scaled and cratered and damaged and ugly?" I nodded and he continued, "But turn it over and look underneath."

He withdrew his hand and I brought mine closer to my face and turned the shell over. The underside of the shell was opalescent pinks and creams and aquamarines, smooth as glass to the touch and cool. It was beautiful and magical and wonderful.

I rubbed my thumb over the surface again and again, and looked up at Henri.

"I've carried that little thing for years now. I forget where I got it from. I want you to have it now. Your friend may be scarred on top, Cousin, and so is the world, but remember what may lie beneath the surface."

"How did you get so wise, Henri" I asked him, bringing the shell to my cheek and rubbing the smooth surface against my skin.

"Pfff..." he said, "It is merely too much wine. I get sentimental! I will leave you to your sewing, yes?"

He left the room. I picked up the mending once more but found I could not concentrate and gave up after a few minutes. I'd wake early and finish it then.

Noises again, down in the cellars this time. The girl? He stifled a smile at the thought of a visit from her. Perhaps, best to check. He got up and moved from his rooms down through the cellars many floors and into the stone passages, working his way towards the sounds but ever above it. Human beings never looked up, wasn't that the most amazing thing? They were so sure of their superiority on this planet they never imagined something could be above them. Astonishing!

More noises. Too heavy to be the Little Mouse, he thought. This was a man's footfalls. The noises in the Opera House had been diminishing with each passing day. More doors were locked, more windows barred. Eric didn't mind. In fact, he rather liked the peace. At least right now, anyway. He was sick to death of screeching sopranos, foppish male dancers and incompetent business men. Possibly even sick of Paris, itself. It would be time to move on when the hunt for him died down, as it inevitably would when they could not find him.

Although, come to think of it, perhaps it would not. He had spotted his prey and it was that damnable Inspector back again with his plans and drawings, this time coming too close to Eric's refuge for his comfort. He was going to pass right underneath Eric's vantage point in a minute. Frankly, anywhere in the cellars was too close for comfort, Eric thought. He contemplated killing him outright. It would be ridiculously easy, because even this man hadn't looked up. Just pounce as he walked underneath, twist his neck and viola! No more bothersome Inspector. The instinct to rid himself of this obstacle in the form of the Inspector was strong but logic took hold and he checked himself. If this man went missing, it would surely begin a manhunt for him, Eric, of a previously unseen magnitude. Previous attempts to find him had been at best half-hearted as belief in his existence was not universal. The disappearance of another person and this one a gendarme, would shift belief in his direction and make raising a determined posse of more experienced hunters probable. It might not be so easy to escape from that one unscathed. And moreover, he was as sick to death of killing and blood as he was of Paris. All he wanted now was to stay still for a while longer, lick his wounds from his last disastrous attempt at a normal life, and then move on to locations undecided as yet.

Something was going to need to be done about this tenacious detective, but Eric wasn't sure what the answer was, and knew that now was not the time. It's the girl, he thought, both of them, and stifled a bitter laugh at that ironic thought. Christine Daae and the Little Mouse. Would that he had never seen Christine! If he had not, he would not have fallen into the trap of thinking he could ever be loved for himself, could ever live a normal life and be someone. He would never have felt *that pain of betrayal and the loss of his self control that came with it. He felt impotent rage wash over him, but knew this was unfair. It was his own actions under it all that had brought this plague upon him. That and the general unjustness of life. It was sheer dumb luck that one of the fuses had not lit properly and he had recovered his control enough to prevent the entire arsenal of gunpowder filled barrels from going up or the entire place and all within would have been blown to bits. And now this mousey little girl was insinuating herself into his world and he was finding himself drawn in by it. Damnation! What catastrophe was this new development going to end with?*

He hovered, waiting for the Inspector to pass by, completely oblivious to how close he had just come to his mortality. When the Inspector's torch had dimmed to nothing and all was dark and still again, Eric swung himself down and disappeared into the gloom the other way, silently cursing policemen, women, the city, and himself most of all.

Six

I was away like a musket shot as soon as possible the next day. The shell sat heavy as a brick in my pocket, and with it the knowledge of my reluctantly admitted to feelings for Eric, a man I had, at best, no right to have such tenderness for. At worst, my feelings could be construed as deranged, unbalanced and very, very dangerous. I had lay awake most of the night, staring at the roof of my little cabinet, feeling the hardness of the floor through the pallet, interrogating myself mercilessly over and over. I had finally fallen into an exhausted and dreamless sleep, from which I'd awoken a few hours later foggy headed and achy.

Many cups of tea later, served by the amiable cook in the kitchens, and I had forced my mind to focus, finished the work left from the day before, flew through my share of the day's laundry and taken my leave of the Gaudet household.

I circled the Opera House twice, carefully checking all sides and my path before deciding I was not followed. I ducked into my usual spot behind the hedge and made my way down to the vaults.

I heard the instrument long before I reached Eric's chambers. The dusty organ, now restored thanks to my careful cleaning, echoed distantly through the cellars. Its distinctive sound drew me like a trail of crumbs to where Eric played. I stepped into the room and spoke his name quietly. I wasn't sure he could hear me above the organ's sonorous notes, but he must have for he halted abruptly with a small smack of his hands on the keys. The discordant note filled the air around us, seeming to last forever as it bounced from one stone wall to another.

As it died, Eric turned on his bench. His mask was in place, his waistcoat perfect, a cloak over it. There was a vibration coming from him, a rigidity. Something was bothering him.

I asked, "You aren't worried someone might hear you? The Inspector?"

"Not at the moment. He is gone. The Opera House is empty." His voice was flat. And then he barked a harsh laugh, "Except for you, of course." He looked at his hands. "And myself."

"It was beautiful. Would you play again?" I asked. Anything to release this predatory tension I sensed.

"No," he said.

"Please?"

"No. Little Mouse, why do you plague me?"

"I'm not plaguing you. Don't play if you don't care to."

He didn't respond, just turned on his bench again, away from me. "Eric, what has happened? What's bothering you? You're not yourself."

"Is that so?" he snarled at me. "You are mistaken, my dear. I am precisely myself. This is me, this!" He growled, stalking me across the room like the leopard from Louis's menagerie I'd imagined him to be. "A madman, an animal, a beast to be hunted down and destroyed. The phantom genius, a decayed monster. A trophy for honest men to display on their walls, to make them feel more of a man. This is who you have chosen to play your game of confidant to, foolish Little Mouse."

I wished he would shout, or throw something. This deadly quiet speech was infinitely more frightening than if he had just lost his temper and raged.

"Why are you trying to frighten me?" I asked quietly.

"Your Inspector was here again, and this time he has found his way to the Opera vaults. My position here has just become several degrees more tenuous," he spat.

"Oh no," I murmured.

"Oh yes. The monster must be flushed from his dungeon once again to be stoned for the public's entertainment." His voice was bitter and hard. I felt tears prick my eyelids at the pain I heard in his voice.

I went to him, fingering the shell in my pocket. "Eric, listen. Eric, you are not a monster." I went to his side and laid a hand on his arm, the sinews were taut underneath the cambric of his shirt. He looked down at me and there was no gentleness in his gaze. Only pain and years of torment.

I took the shell from my pocket and held it up. "Look, look at this. It's a shell. Henri, my cousin, he gave it to me. Look at the outside of it, Eric."

I took his hand, that strong hand with long narrow fingers. A musician's hand. I opened his fist and placed the shell in his palm. I did not let go his hand. He didn't pull away.

"See how plain and scarred it is? Rough and worn by the sea? The cruel, unfeeling sea? But turn it over Eric, look at the other side." I reached out and gently turned the shell over in Eric's palm. I pressed my thumb to the center of the shell, pushing it gently into the center of his hand. My other fingers came around to cup the back of Eric's hand in my own. I felt the heat of his skin against my palm. I looked into his eyes and saw myself reflected in them.

"Beneath the ugliness, Eric, lies beauty," I said softly. Still I did not release his hand. My breath came shallow, my heart beat as slowly as treacle. I thought then that I would die from love. Oh, please, I breathed silently into the stillness, please stay with me. Don't be that man you don't want to be. I took his thumb in my other hand and rubbed it softly across the satiny interior of the shell, felt him watching our hands moving together across the iridescent surface.

Abruptly, he pushed me away from him and threw the shell to the ground. It skittered across the floor and came up against a candelabrum. He slammed his fist into the table near where we stood. I heard the wood crack. "Damn you! Why are you tormenting me?" he shouted.

"I'm not. You don't have to show yourself every time I come here. You never did." I said to his back as he stormed around the room. I wanted to cry. I didn't dare to.

He flew across the room and grabbed my arm roughly. I squeaked in protest.

"LEAVE ME IN PEACE!"

His shout echoed off the rock, mocking us once, twice and one more time, "...in peace..."

I felt the blood drain from my face, and the world stood still. My vision narrowed until all I could see was the vein pulsing at his neck, the flush on his skin, the rise and fall of his chest with each breath. His grip on my upper arm loosened but he did not let go, not completely. I felt my treasonous lip quiver, and dropped my head from his face to hide it. I saw my invisible, interior wall coming back up around me, felt it...and did nothing to stop it. I was helpless.

Numbly I whispered, "Of course," and stepped away, out of his grasp. I crept over to the candelabra to retrieve the shell. I picked it up, held it a moment, then set it down meaningfully on the table. Without looking at Eric, I left.

Seven

At the Gaudet's home that evening I sat to dinner with the other household servants, listening to the idle chatter and hearing none of it. I ate little, and when Henri asked me if I was feeling well, I barely managed a quiet murmur of assent and a small nod before claiming exhaustion and escaping to the comfort of my pallet. I could feel his eyes on my back as I left the room, and knew I'd need to answer his questions at some point. That was a conversation for another day, however. I couldn't bear it tonight. I'd fall to pieces. I felt stuck together with thin paste, like the sticky sap inside some flowers I'd play with as a child, making crowns of daisy petals that mostly fell apart in a matter of hours. So I crawled into my pallet and slept, and slept. In the morning I could not bring myself to get out of bed, not even when another maid, Marie, came and shook me. It did not seem to matter even if I were to be dismissed from my post and sent back to my mother's house. Amelie declared me unwell and feverish and bade me stay to my bed. I hugged my wrap and gloves to me, the gifts from Eric, still faintly smelling of his scent, pressed against my cheek. The other maids were solicitous save for one, Georgette, who resented that my work should now fall to her. I didn't care. It didn't matter.

When I awoke on the morning of the second day, I sat up on my pallet, tucked the wool gloves and wrap down under the pallet as far as they would go, and got up. I went downstairs and without a word to anyone, resumed my duties. I was correct about Henri wanting to talk, as he attempted it that afternoon, but I would have none of it. I shrugged him off and he chose wisely not to pester me. I had no reason to leave the house that day and so I finished my work and asked Georgette if I could help her with hers to make up for my absence the day before. She allowed me to with ill humor, but by the time we had finished she was her normal self again, which if I am to be honest, was not all that much better. I had dinner in the kitchens with the other staff, and went to bed.

Thus my days passed, one flowing into another without my noticing their passing. Armand continued to lurk about the streets, but as I had no need to leave the grounds, he didn't even signify in my shrunken world.

The news sheets that M. Gaudet brought home and that passed to the upper servants when he was through and then down to us occasionally carried news of the continued closure of the Opera House and investigation that was still on for the purported Opera Ghost. As the days and soon weeks passed, the news stories started to sound more and more doubtful that such a creature existed. I tried as hard as I might to pay no attention to these stories, but in the way of human beings everywhere I could not resist their pull and I read every one, then hated myself for it afterwards. He was safe, at least, or had not been caught anyway, and I knew myself to be glad of it, even as I chided myself for caring one way or another.

The days grew colder and still I did not take my wrap and gloves from under my pallet. My hands grew red and chapped. The harsh water and scrubbing of the laundries had always been hard on them of course, but now the cold air when I was not washing made it doubly so. At night Amelie bade me rub goose grease into them. It seemed to help, and in the morning they'd be a little better, only to grow worse again as I worked throughout the day.

I felt no need to leave the house, and did so only on the urging of someone else to fetch some bread or another household errand no one else had time to do. On these occasional outings I took great pains to avoid the sly Armand. It took much planning however, for he seemed to delight in waiting for days for me to emerge. Even Amelie and Henri and the other servants noticed my distress and the requests for me to run errands lessened because of it.

And so I was home, sitting outside in the chill, taking advantage of the last of the light of the day to finish a hem on one of M. Gaudet's frockcoats, when a familiar face appeared at the gate.

I looked up to see the loathsome Inspector Bruyere smiling at me.

"Mademoiselle," he greeted. "Good day to you. I have not seen you about the neighborhood for some weeks."

I didn't answer. What could I say after all? That he had not seen me about because I had not been about and that I held him largely responsible for this turn of events? I held my tongue and waited. I'd gotten quite good once again at holding my tongue and waiting over the last few weeks.

"Catching the last of the day's light?" he asked.

I nodded. "It is easier on the eyes to work in sunlight."

"Clever of you to do so. The days are growing shorter, soon it will be too cold to work outside, I am sure."

"Yes," I said.

"Speaking of work, work will be starting soon on the reparation of the Opera Garnier. Had you heard? Is that not good news?" he said.

"I had not heard, no," I said and declined to comment on the concept of it being good news or no. I wasn't entirely sure actually.

"Will you be returning to it once it re-opens?" he asked conversationally.

This was one of the bizarrer discussions I'd ever had with someone. On the face of it, he was just chatting with me about a subject of mutual interest. And in the listening I truly could not hear any underlying motive to his questions. Yet I knew there must be one. What could it possibly be? I wondered. I had not been to the Opera House in weeks. What information could I possibly have for him now? I wished he would just leave me in peace. As the thought entered my mind I remembered the echo on the rocks of the underground lake of those same words. The pain I'd been burying came back to me in a rush. I struggled to hide it.

The Inspector carried on without waiting for an answer from me as to my return to the Opera. "Of course, they will be draining that lake down below and filling in the cellars. That's the first step in the restoration. They are outdated and unsafe, everyone has finally come to realize. Who knows what sort of pestilence has been breeding in that water, and what sort of cut-throats could be hiding down there."

I felt the blood drain from my face but did not react. I was wise enough to know that he'd finally gotten to the point, which was to shock me into some sort of action. I hated to disappoint him, but I was not going to be baited, nor be the bait to catch the 'cutthroat' I knew he really wanted.

"I am sure you are correct, Inspector," I replied. "One would not want anything or anyone below the Opera House that did not belong there," I said sincerely but pointedly.

He did not miss my meaning and smiled. "No, one would surely not, Mademoiselle."

Game point to me.

"Well, I do not wish to keep you from your work. It seems the light is fading, and I can see you are not finished with your stitching. I will wish you *bon soir*, Mademoiselle. I look forward to our next meeting."

"Do you think we will be meeting again, Inspector?" I asked demurely.

He smiled that wolf-like smile, "I am quite sure of it, Mademoiselle. *Au revoir*."

"*Au revoir*, Inspector," I said and turned my attention back to my sewing, hoping the shaking of my hands did not show as I stabbed the needle into the coat.

He watched me a few seconds more as I stitched, then turned and walked away down the street. I sewed on for a bit, and then, when I was sure he was gone, ripped out all the stitches. They were completely crooked.

Eric lit the flame and watched while the kindling took. In a moment a small fire that should have been cheery was burning in the pit he'd made out of a depression in the stone near the edge of the lake. When it was going well he laid the wax head on top of the flames and watched as it began to melt, the wax dripping, reminding him alarmingly of his own damaged face. He barked a small bitter laugh then. If Christine only knew how little separated them in the end. All would melt away eventually. He could have her, the love-struck swain, that pathetic nobleman. The Little Mouse was right, Christine Daae would have been destroyed living a life with him, and all he'd loved in her would have been ruined. And then what? Would he have cast her out? Abandoned her? Or kept her locked away till she'd grown as mad as he and withered away?

The fire was smoking heavily. The smell of wax was strong, and unpleasant. Eric got up and moved far enough away that the melting figure wouldn't bother him, then stood and watched the flames. He was going to have to make some decisions soon, he thought. This place was no longer a real refuge, and it was merely a matter of time before he'd be flushed out. He'd slowly begun some preparations for erasing his existence here, thus the burning of the wax figure, though that served another purpose as well: ridding him of her memory, he hoped. The rest of the doll had been dumped with some solemnity in the Seine days ago along with some various other unnecessary items. His small boat had been partly reconfigured and moved to a quiet dock at the River. Some drawings and notes had been burned already. He had a short list of places to retreat to: other cities, other countries, places he could disappear into. The Orient perhaps? Maybe America? One could truly disappear into the wilds there. Or south to Greece or Rome... The final choosing of one he kept putting off because that would mean there would be no real excuse not to attempt to book passage to it. And he found he could not quite bring himself to leave. Not yet. He kept waiting. Waiting for her to come back. Not Christine, surprisingly, the Little Mouse. Sophie.

The girl hadn't come in weeks now. Weeks. He assumed he'd frightened her off with his tirade. He had regretted it almost the minute the harsh words begging her leave him alone were out, but hadn't known how to take them back. She was not really bothering him. He rather enjoyed the company and had looked forward to her visits, the realization of which had completely surprised him, but there you have it. Whether he appreciated the company or not was now a moot point as she was not likely to ever return now.

The flames reflecting off the rocks reminded him of the candle flames in her slanted almond shaped eyes, turning their tawny color honey gold, and how her full bottom lip had quivered though she had fought to hide it from him. He had hurt her, and the knowledge was a heavy burden. After a week, when it had become clear to him that she was not *coming back any time soon, he'd explored the idea of trying to find her. What he'd do with her once he did he had no earthly idea, but he'd cross that hurdle when he came to it. Finding her had proved impossible a task so far. He'd hung about the rooftops and balconies, thinking to maybe catch a glimpse of her on the street on some errand. Nothing. And the continued intrusive presence of the Inspector made being out in the open, even on the roof, somewhat risky. He abandoned that for trying to recall where she may live, but the only thing he could come up with was the name of her...cousin, was it? Henri? How many Henri's were there in Paris? Hundreds? Thousands? She had to be in the area or she'd not have been able to be at the Opera House so often, but the knowledge of her proximity did nothing when he could think of no way to find her. She may as well have been on the moon. He had made the mistake of not asking her too many questions about herself. A mistake he wished now he could rectify. The little minx had outwitted him. A rare event and something he was far from accustomed to, or accepting of. It was this which kept him here at the Opera House long after it had outgrown its usefulness. He couldn't quite bring himself to give up.*

He didn't want to be alone again.

I held out another eight days, but Inspector Bruyere's words had cracked the shell I'd painstakingly erected around my heart. My concern for Eric and my own desire to see him won and I decided to visit the Opera House one more time. I didn't even know if he were still there. After a moment's thought I left my wrap and gloves behind. On the afternoon I'd chosen, I took a meandering path from the Gaudet's very late in the day, hoping not to run afoul of the horrid Armand if I were partly in shadow, and hoping that an indirect path would throw off the Inspector should he be observing my movements. I kept a hood over my tell-tale hair and took my time, dawdling in shop windows, and checking guiltily over my shoulders even though I tried so hard not to. It felt like history repeating itself as I stood in the doorway of a closed patisserie observing the great building from across the street. It was very quiet. No carriages, no pedestrians walking about it, no lights inside, nothing. There was a tremulous fluttering in my stomach as I moved around the building from shadow to shadow, and near to my friend, the hedge. A quick look about, a dash and I was behind the hedge and through the access door, my heart pounding. I rested just inside the little doorway, listening for sounds of anyone following me behind the hedge. Several minutes passed. Nothing. Finally, I decided I was as safe as I could be, and I moved into the Opera House making my way down to the cellars and Eric's rooms.

I made pains to make noise once I got to the bottom of the rotunda. Not loud ones, but enough that he would hear me through the elaborate acoustical system he had created in the building. If he would see me, I hoped to give him clear notice that I was there. If he would not, I wanted to give him enough time to disappear in order to prevent another repeat of the last time I'd been down here.

"Eric?" I said softly into the empty gloom as I made my way through the corridors.

A quiet sound in the passages made him lift his head sharply. He'd been lying on his back on his bed, a canopied,

heavily carved monstrosity draped in silk, staring at the ceiling of his apartments, thinking of her yet again and turning the scrap of shell she had left behind over and over in his fingertips. And now, as if his thoughts had magicked her here, her voice and the sound of her footsteps drifted through the air to him.

At last! He leapt up and grabbing his mask, flew from the room.

I stepped into the room a second before he did. His mask was in place, as always, but otherwise he seemed unprepared. His shirt was unbuttoned down almost to his waist, his feet were bare and his hair was loose round his shoulders. My heart swelled. Damned treacherous heart! Damned treacherous eyes, I felt them burning with tears.

We neither of us said anything for a moment, just looked at one another, then he ran a hand through his hair, as though he was not sure what to do with his hands and said, "Sophie."

It was the first time I had heard him speak my name and the last vestiges of the egg shell round my heart fell away. I was lost. Heaven help me. What I would do if he rejected me again, I did not know.

"Eric," I said.

We lapsed back into silence.

A moment passed then he said, "I am sorry."

And just like that, everything was all right again. What magic words, those. They can erase the most painful of events just in the speaking of them if said sincerely.

"Don't go away like that again, please," he asked.

I shook my head. "I won't."

I knew in some distant recess of my mind that decorum demanded I stay where I was, but I took two steps towards him, and then he was moving swiftly across the room towards me. He stopped a foot from me. I rested my hand against a bookshelf near me, trying to keep myself steady. I felt our breath match one another. He slid a hand into the pocket of his trousers and withdrew Henri's shell. He held it up between us, the smooth beautiful side towards me, close enough to my face I had to cross my eyes slightly for it to swim into clarity. I shifted my focus back to his eyes. He raised an eyebrow as though asking if I understood his meaning. This side of the shell was perfect. Satisfied that I had gotten the message, he abruptly turned the shell over, revealing the ugly scarred side of it to my view. I glanced at it, and back to him

"This is the side the world sees, Sophie, this wreck of a carcass, this destroyed monster. This is my face and so, my fate. You understand? It will never change."

"It is a scar Eric, just a scar, something life marked you with, like the color of your eyes or the shape of your hands. Your soul does not create your scars, and you do not have to let your scars create your soul." My tongue was beginning to run away with me again. I was so desperate to have him see what I knew to be true.

"Your scars do not scare me, Eric. Everyone has scars. Yours are just more visible than most, but everyone has them. See? Look!" and before I thought what I was doing, I lifted my toe to one of the lower shelves of the bookcase I'd been holding on to and pulled my skirts up just past my knee. A vivid pink, puckered gash about three inches long garishly decorated my thigh about two inches above the knee.

"A mishap a few years ago with a fabric scissors. It healed poorly. A scar, Eric. Ugly, but underneath, my leg works just the same and it altered me not a whit, except that I grew more cautious with the scissors." I finished my speech with a brief ironic laugh.

I looked from my leg towards him. His eyes were riveted on my thigh as though bound there with chain. I felt the blood flood swiftly up my neck and over my face. I had been so caught up that every nuance of propriety had utterly fled me. What must he think of my spectacle! I hastily shoved my skirts back down and dropped my leg to the floor once more.

The movement must have broken the enchantment. He muttered, "A scar."

"Yes," I said soothingly. He looked at my face, searching for the truth in my words. "Just a scar," I repeated.

Hesitantly I put my two hands on either side of his head. My left hand stroked the smoothness of his mask, the other, the warmth of the undamaged side of his face. His eyes blinked closed, shutting away from me the years of pain I could read there. He leaned his head into my right palm slightly.

"Eric, your mask..." I put my left hand to the mask but didn't pull it away, waiting. His hands shot out and grabbed my arms, stilling me.

"No," he commanded.

"It's okay, Eric, let me see. I'm not frightened."

A short tiny nod of his head I took to be a nervous assent and I slipped my thumb under the mask and lifted gently. His breath came fast and short. I lifted more and drew away the mask.

How can I describe what I saw? His beloved face, dead looking grey flesh, intersected by red angry pockmarks. Skin blistered and raw, scarred, drawn together as though knitted by a crazed demon, the hairline pulled away from the charred forehead, the right eye drooping.

I couldn't stop a small cry of anguish.

Instantly, Eric stiffened and abruptly pulled away, grabbing his mask and turning from me, meaning to replace it over his torn features. I reached out and swiftly grabbed his hand. "No, no, it is only sorrow for your suffering! It's allright, Eric, please. It's allright."

He turned back to me. I let go his hand and reached for the scarred side of his face. He flinched but held still and I lightly touched the ruined flesh with my fingertips, tracing the contours of the old wounds. Following a nurturing instinct as old as woman-kind I stood on my tiptoes and stretched up to his ruined cheek, pressing my lips gently to the flesh there.

I pulled my head back. "Just scars."

And then he kissed me. No dramatic kiss from one of the scandalous popular ladies novels, this, no, just a simple meeting of two sets of lips, an exploration of the possibility of meeting again for more. It was sweet and tender and when we pulled apart I breathed a sigh and out with it went all the pent up longing and loneliness of my life. I fluttered my eyes open. Eric's eyes were still closed, the lashes glistening. His arms went around me and he squeezed me tight against him then kissed me again. This one was longer and harder and time seemed to stop. I was acutely aware of the heat of him against me, and the pulse beating in the hollow of his throat. My fingertips drifted like a minnow through the soft hairs on his chest. His muscles there flexed and his arms tightened even more. Isn't it strange the way time can feel as though it has stopped and nothing at all is moving outside the tiny bubble you are floating in. Then all at once, the bubble drifts to earth and pops on a blade of grass and time suddenly rushes forward to catch up with itself and you find yourself wondering what happened and where it all went?

I left The Opera House soon after, my lips bruised and heart full, and absolutely no idea of what we would do next. That nothing could be easy was certain, but for tonight, I would just revel in the feeling of wanting and being wanted in return. I was so giddy I didn't pay as much attention as usual to my route and I never even noticed Armand.

But he noticed me.

Eight

I turned a corner and ran smack into him, coming up against his chest with a whuff of surprise and staggering to a halt. His arms went right up, steadying me, but did not let go once I'd regained my footing. He seemed as surprised as I was by the meeting. So, he had not been lying in wait for me at least, small comfort that the knowledge was. He recovered his aplomb faster than I though. He slid both arms around my waist and pulled me closer.

"Hello, pretty thing!" he cooed, like a man who had just won a prize he hadn't expected.

I leaned away as far as his aching grip would allow. "Let me go."

"You've been hiding," he said. "I missed you." He squeezed me tighter.

"Please, let me go."

"A kiss. Give me a kiss, and I'll let you go," he said.

I shook my head hard and pushed against him.

"Stop fighting, girl," he growled and his voice grew cold.

I didn't stop fighting. I couldn't. Flashes of memory, sharp as knife blades tore through me. Another man, holding me tight telling me to give him a kiss. My panicked mind played tricks on my eyes, making them alternately see Armand's face one instant and the other man's in the next. One arm dropped from me, but in the next instant before I could squirm away a hand was forced roughly between my legs.

I screamed then. I screamed and screamed and felt a hard fist against my face, knocking my head sideways and wrenching my neck. Everything went momentarily black, and Armand took advantage of this cessation of my struggles to drop his face to mine and stop any more screaming with his mouth. I fought desperately, squealing behind my lips as his tongue pushed itself between my teeth then registered something black, like an enormous bat dropping from the roof of the nearest shop and landing directly behind Armand.

Suddenly Armand disappeared as he was pulled backwards away from me and thrown to the ground. Standing above him was Eric, an avenging angel in a black cloak and hood. The hood had fallen back during his leap from the roof revealing his mask and face. There was a dark murderous rage there. Armand made to stand and Eric leapt on him and drove a fist into his face, breaking the other man's nose with a sound like that of a host of snails being crushed.

I stood frozen, relief and terror battling it out within me.

Eric hit Armand again and once again and then pulled the other man up by the collar and looked to be preparing to smash his head into the cobbles.

Relief won. I unfroze,

"No! Eric, no, stop!" at my cry he paused, but did not take his eyes off his prey, "Don't kill him. It will be you they hunt. Please, please, stop."

Time froze again for the second time that day. Armand lay senseless and bloody in Eric's hands, moaning. Eric didn't move, just kneeled with his knee in the other man's chest, holding his shirt in his two hands. I didn't dare move either, not until he decided whether or not to listen to my pleas.

When the clock ticked again, Eric roughly dropped Armand, stood off of him and turned to me. "Mercy then, for the wicked," he said finally. "For your sake."

I went to him then and wrapped my arms around him, pressing my face into his chest. He held me a moment, and let me burrow under his chin, but the predator side was not finished. He felt drawn tight. I thought that if I plucked at his arm, it would twang like an violin. To our left, Armand crawled into the shadows of the shop door.

"No man will ever touch you like that again, I swear it. Or they will die," Eric growled. He lifted my chin and looked at my face, taking my chin in his hand and turning it to the streetlamp. His brows drew down at whatever he saw, and he made a sound deep in his throat. "I swear it," he repeated. A moment of thought and some decision I was not privy to made he drew his hood up to hide his mask, took me by the arm and pulled me quickly down the street.

I was somewhat pressed to keep up with his long strides, but I dared not complain. Not while the predator was in him. He would not hurt me; I felt no fear at all for my own safety now. Not from him and certainly not from anything else now he was with me. But he was intent, so very focused and I was not sure he would not change his mind about killing Armand and turn back if I interrupted him. So I hurried alongside him, occasionally needing to trot a few steps to match his stride.

He stopped suddenly. "Where are we going?" he asked.

The question took me so completely by surprise, I couldn't think of an answer, "What? I...where...but you...Going? How should I know?"

He looked down at me, his face in shadows under his hood. His one unmasked eye shone out like a cat's. "Your home, where is it?"

I pointed like an idiot, "There, just up the street and round the next corner to the right, on Rue Valciennes."

He turned and started up the street again, towing me along like a child's little boat behind a great ship.

"Where did you come from?" I asked.

"I followed you from the Opera House."

"You...followed me? Why ever for?" Events were happening rather too fast for me. It seemed my brain could not quite keep pace for nothing was making any sense.

"Because the last time you left, you did not return for well over a month and I had no way to go find you myself. I was not going to let that happen again," he said.

"Oh. Oh, yes, for sure." Somewhere inside of me a hopeless romantic teenage girl was swooning with glee over this bit of information. The almost-old-maid I'd grown into was not sure how to respond.

"And it appears that it is a fine thing I did follow you," he said wryly. "How often has he accosted you like that?"

"Like that? Never before. He has been a terrible pest though ever since I came here after the fire."

Eric growled in the back of his throat. "You should have let me kill him."

"No"

"He deserves it."

"They would have hunted you for a murderer."

He stopped then and turned to me, taking both my arms in his hands, "They already hunt me for a murderer, Sophie. I *am* a murderer."

We started walking again. I was silent while I processed this and then said, "Then why did you stop from killing him?"

"Because you asked it of me."

I had nothing to say to that.

"Gather your things," Eric ordered as we turned into the Gaudet's walk.

"My things?" I asked, bewildered. "You are not seeing me home?"

"You are coming back to the Opera House with me."

"I am? Oh, I am! All right, I'll go quickly, but thats what I came to the Opera House today to tell you! I'd entirely forgotten with, well with everything. Inspector Bruyere was here a week ago. He says they are going to begin work there and are going to drain the lake and clear out the cellars! You can't stay there."

Eric didn't reply. A moment while I searched his face and found the answer there and I said, "You already know this don't you?"

"There is very little about my Opera House I don't know. Regardless, do not trouble yourself. We will not stay there long. I have made some plans. But tonight you need to rest."

Reassured, I said, "I have to tell Henri I am leaving. He will worry if I don't. What are you going to do?"

He took a mysterious moment before answering and then just said, "I will be here when you return. Go now, don't delay."

I turned and hurried up the steps to the servant's entrance and went into the house.

Without even stopping a moment to consider the complete impropriety of what I was about to do and the effect it would certainly have on my reputation and my employment, and therefore my very life, I hurried up the back stairs towards the servants' quarters. I ran into Georgette on the way.

"Henri," I asked her, "Where is he? Is he here?"

"*Oui*, I think so," she answered sullenly and then she spotted something about me that made her mouth drop and her eyebrows rise.

"Where? Please Georgette, I am in a hurry," I begged.

Still staring at my cheek, she pointed down the hall. "He was on the landing when I came down."

I pushed past her and climbed the three floors up to the servants' quarters at a jog. As I neared the top I called, "Henri? Henri." He was almost to his room, but he turned as I made my way down the hall.

"Sophie! You are out of breath. Has something happened? Good God! What happened to your face?"

My hand flew to my cheek. I had forgotten about it. That must be what had stopped Georgette. "It's nothing, Henri. Armand, he grabbed me and hit me when I wouldn't kiss him."

"That bastard! I'll kill him!" Henri exclaimed.

"No, no, Henri, it's all right. My friend, you remember my friend? He was following and he...stopped him. I'm fine, it's just a bruise, nothing more. But Henri, please... No darling, really...I'm fine. I don't think Armand will be bothering me again...Henri, please, I must tell you something! I'm leaving."

That got through his chivalrous anger and he stopped and turned to me. "What?"

"I'm leaving. I'm going with my friend. He wants me to be with him."

"Are you mad? Is he? What does he propose? That you destroy your reputation and your life and play mistress to him? Who is this insane person?" he demanded.

"Henri, if I tell you, you must promise, as my Cousin, as my best friend, not to tell ever. Once you know, you'll understand. Please, Henri," I pleaded.

He nodded but I could see he was reserving judgment.

"You have heard of the Opera Ghost?"

"Are you completely out of your wits, Sophie?" he roared, loudly enough that several faces peeped out of doors. Then he shook me, as if that might instill me with common sense.

I laughed, most likely a hysterical one, after the evening's events. "Yes! Yes, Henri! I think I am!" I couldn't think of anything else to say, so I just turned towards my cabinet and walked away from him.

He stood staring after me a moment, then followed.

I reached my cabinet and started gathering my few things. My gloves and wrap, which I put on, and the very few other things I had managed to acquire: a comb, a change of underthings, some stockings, my hood, and other small similar items.

"Sophie, why are you doing this?" Henri asked, angry.

I bundled my things into my spare petticoat and tied it together with the black silk ribbon from Eric's gift. It made a pitifully small bundle.

I looked at him and stood. "I love him, Henri."

"I forbid this!" he ordered.

I put my hand to his cheek. "Henri, I have taken your advice and opened my heart. Now I have to follow it. I love you!"

And I hurried away from him down the stairs towards the garden, leaving him speechless and standing watching me go.

He watched until she was in the house, then he moved swiftly round, peering in windows and testing doors. He found what he wanted, an unlatched window into a dark, empty room and went in. Moving swiftly, he began searching the house, silently hunting his prey.

It wasn't long before he found it. There in what he assumed was a man's study was an older gentleman, sitting stiffly in dinner jacket and trousers, sipping some drink of an amber color -brandy probably- and going over some pile of papers and reports. His back was to the door, so Eric slipped in unseen and moved through the shadows to the other side of the room. He waited a moment.

Just as the man lifted his snifter towards his lips, Eric said, "The care you take for the women in your household is deplorable."

The snifter flew from the man's hands and crashed to the rug, spilling its contents. The sharp smell of brandy rose into the air. Timing was everything, The Phantom thought, and could be very amusing when used to its proper effect. M. Gaudet leapt from his chair with a cry, knocking it backwards. He spun, trying to locate, unsuccessfully, the voice in the darkness. Eric let him flounder a bit then stepped into the edges of the meager light from the lamp. He kept his hood over his face, hiding his mask from view.

"Good God in heaven, man! Are you trying to kill me? Who are you?" M. Gaudet demanded, a hand to his chest.

"Are you aware that a common footpad has assaulted one of your maids this evening and has been harassing her for weeks?" Eric asked, his voice low and threatening.

"Is the girl all right?" M. Gaudet asked.

Eric made a low sound of assent

"There you are, then. It's dreadfully unfortunate, but it is the concern of the Butler and Housekeeper, not mine. Who are you?" he repeated.

Eric stepped into the light and removed his hood. Monsieur Gaudet inhaled sharply and took a step back, nearly tripping over the fallen chair. "What are you?"

"I, Monsieur, am the Phantom of the Opera. See that you make it your concern from this day forth, do I make myself *quite clear?" he advanced on the older man, who nodded quickly.*

"The maid, Sophie, is leaving your employ as of this evening." He took a handful of coins from his pocket. These he tossed onto the floor at Monsieur Gaudet's feet. He nodded at them, "Compensation, for the loss of your maid."

With that, he stepped back into the shadows, and slipped from the room. Making his way to the back of the house he spotted Sophie coming down the stairs followed by a young man. The cousin, he assumed, the resemblance was unmistakable as they both had the same multicolored hair. He was chastising her for something. Eric could guess what it was, but she was standing firm against him. His brave Little Mouse! He watched her hug the man once more then head for the kitchen door. He turned and made his own way back out.

Eric was waiting by the gate when I returned to him. He took my small bundle of belongings, put a hand out to pull my wrap more closely about my body -I had started shivering- and took my arm, pulling me once more down the street. Keeping to shadows, we hurried back towards the Opera House.

Once there, out of habit, I headed towards my entrance under the hedge, but Eric stopped and said, "Not that way."

"But the grate under the hedge is back this way. That's how I always get in." It hadn't occurred to me to wonder how he had gotten *out*, but it did then. "What way do you go?"

He smiled, but said nothing and led me to the very rear of the Opera House. There, in between two narrow wings of the building, was a drain from the roof. He reached into the crevice and came away with a rope in his hand. He gave me my bundle, put an arm around me and said, "Hold on," then hit a brick in the wall with his fist.

The floor gave way under us, as an invisible trap door opened and swung away. We dropped like stones. I squeaked, in alarm, but before I could even bury my face in his chest we had landed. I looked up to where we had fallen from. The opening was no more than 10 feet above us and through it I could see the Paris sky and the walls of the Opera House. Eric tied the rope to a cleat in the wall, making it appear to be nothing more than some piece of a clever stage mechanism, and then moved to one side and lifted a lever. The trap door above swung back up on some sort of hinge and Paris disappeared.

I looked at him. He looked back and his mouth lifted on one side

"Better than a grate under a bush, isn't it?"

"Rather ostentatious, actually."

He laughed. "Come."

I was only familiar with about half of the passages he led me through on our way to the cellars, but assumed we were going to his lair. It surprised me then when he headed down another level past this, grabbing a torch from the wall on our way and lighting it with a match from his pocket. "Wait," I said. "This is too far. This isn't where your chambers are."

"We can't go there. They'll be coming for me for certain very soon, and they will go there first. They found it the night of the fire, you remember?"

I'm not sure why I had not realized that. I was perhaps over tired and not thinking. Of course those rooms would not be safe any longer. But then…? "So, you have not been staying there all this time have you?" I asked.

He shook his head. "No."

"Where have you been then?"

"Here," he said and pushed a stone in the wall. A portion of the stone the height of a man rolled to one side an inch. He pushed it and it rolled open sideways enough to permit us passage through it. With a hand on the small of my back he ushered me into the room. Leaving me at the door, he went into the room with the torch to a gas lamp. Lighting this he turned up the flame and I took my first look at his current home.

Rather than the series of small rooms of the other lair, this one was one largish oddly shaped room. The walls were of stone, and draped with hangings of a deep blue and silver. There was a massive canopied bed against the wall to our right, a real one, not the coffin shaped folly from his other lair. There was a trunk at the foot of this, and an armoire opposite. A baby grand piano and piano stool stood to our left nearest us. A table of some foreign wood I did not recognize stood against the far wall with a chair with carved legs. A multi-partitioned screen carved of the same wood was in a corner and over the top of it was a dressing gown in black. More candelabras and here and there a few gas lamps stood on the floor and on other tables and a desk to the left nearest the door. An enormous mirror, easily eight foot high, dominated the space, even more so than the elaborate bed. It stood against the wall to the right of the door.

I moved into the room. The events of the last several hours were really beginning to catch up with me. Here in this place where I felt at last I could rest, I relaxed my guard and found my knees felt weak and my mind utterly exhausted. I wasn't sure how much longer I could stand. I moved to a chair and sat at the edge of it. My corset pinched, the boning digging into my armpits as I sagged.

Eric meanwhile was prowling around the room like Louis's leopard again. The predator was still on the hunt. He was wound and pacing, looking for something, I thought.

He found it for he pulled a low chest from somewhere deep in the bottom of the armoire and carried it to the desk where he set it down with a thud that shook the table. Fitting a key to its lock, he turned it and flung open the lid then started rummaging through the contents. I could not see what was in the chest, his back was in front of it, but he must have gotten what he wanted from it, because with a satisfied grunt he held his arm to his face and pivoted on his heels. Moving across the room he stood in front of me and held out his hand.

I shifted my eyes to it and he opened his fist. There in his palm was a ring. It was very clearly a man's ring, in gold, with an intricately worked woven design to the wide band and a stone of blue set into the center.

I looked back up at him inquiringly. He gestured to me to take it from him.

I did and turned it over in my fingers. I watched and waited while he paced round the room. Eventually he came to me and dropped to his knees in front of me.

"Eric. Is this…are you…are you proposing marriage to me?"

"Did you think I would keep you as a concubine?"

As I had not thought much about it at all, I said nothing.

"It's the smallest I have," he held up a fist, the smallest finger pointed to the ceiling. "It's meant for a man's last finger. You will have whatever you like, but this must do for now."

Things were happening so fast. I shook my head slightly, but fitted the ring onto each finger in turn. On my thumb it was bulky and awkward but would not slip off. I left it there.

"This is the strangest proposal ever made, I think. Why are you asking me now?" I asked.

"I thought it best to seal the bargain before you had a chance to think too hard upon it," he said sarcastically, and gave me a small smile. He grew serious again. "I can't stay here much longer, Sophie. I have to leave Paris, probably by morning after this evening's events. I would take you with me, but I would not ask you to leave all you know as anything less than a wife. I am a damaged man, Sophie, deformed in body and soul. Life with me would not be an easy one, and I will sorely try you, I have no doubt. But you will own me."

I couldn't focus. I was so tired, and overwhelmed, and one part of me was terribly convinced that everything that had happened in the last several hours was merely a dream, or the delirious fantasy of a fever. The glint of the stone on my finger drew my eye and in my exhaustion I felt pulled into it and couldn't take my eyes away. I turned my thumb lazily this way and that.

How much time had passed, I wasn't sure but it may have been some minutes because at last Eric folded his arms across my knees and abruptly buried his head into them, "Sophie, please, don't torment me further. Will you have me?"

"Oh! Yes, of course, I will. Oh Eric, of course!"

Then I was in his arms and he was kissing me again, so hard I could not catch my breath. He tasted of salt and wine. My legs were turning to jelly and the heat from our bodies pressed together was so strong I thought I would melt with it, like molten chocolate inside a croissant from my favorite patisserie. There was this burning within me, a need as strong as air, to somehow defy all laws of reality and mesh my skin, my bones, my soul to his. How did people stand this yearning?

Eric swept me into his arms and carried me, half swooning from desire to the massive bed. He set me down and our hands met at the collar of my blouse, tangling up together but somehow popping each button out of their holes, and pushing the discarded clothing to the floor in a careless pile of fabric then gave his waistcoat and shirt the same careless and hurried treatment. I dropped my hands as he reached around for the ribbons of my corset, untying them agonizingly slowly, slipping his hand smoothly down my skin from neck to collarbone to chest and between the mounds of flesh there that he released as he pulled the garment away. I reached for his mask, looking into his eyes. He put his hands up and cupped my hands in his and together we pulled it away. I pulled his head down to mine and kissed the perfect side of his face, and then the damaged side.

"Sophie," he breathed.

Lowering me down to the cushions, he climbed in beside me. I felt the weight of his desire pressing me down and then I knew no more of the world for a long time. I knew only Eric.

Nine

We lay, my back to his chest, his arm cradling my head, his breath warm on my neck.

"Do you love me?" I asked softly into the hush.

"What?" he asked.

"Do you love me?" I repeated. "You have not said so."

"Do I love you?" He asked, pushing himself to one elbow. I turned my head to look over my shoulder at him. He kissed my shoulder, "I have nearly killed for you and would gladly do it again. I would gladly take my own life for you. Do I love you? More than life." He kissed my shoulder again, slowly and traced a pattern with his tongue. "You taste like honey. I could eat you. The question is: do you love me in return, or am I an answer for you? A way out of drudgery? For clearly you are not born to such a life as you were leading."

"I suspect I have loved you for years," I said. "I was perhaps nineteen, maybe still eighteen, when I saw you the first time, and I loved you then. How not to love a man who is so comfortable swinging about the highest rafters and climbing walls like some hero out of a fairy land? If you do not stop chewing on my arm, I will not have much of it left by morning."

He left off his nipping of my flesh and pressed a kiss to the inside of my elbow. "The watcher becomes the watched. I never saw you. Never even knew you were there, and you've watched me all this time?"

I nodded, "I almost cried out the first time I saw you. I was that shocked to see another person in my secret world. In all the years I'd been wandering behind the walls, I'd never seen anyone. I thought no one else knew of them anymore but me. You were quite a surprise, but I was afraid of you, so I held my tongue. "

"Afraid." he said.

"I'd heard the stories of the Opera Ghost. I was afraid, but I was enchanted as well. So I followed you instead. That's how I knew how to find you after the fire. I saw much. I was hiding, and I saw much of what happened with Christine Daae and The Viscomte. I was on the roof when you were listening to them make their secret engagement thinking to trick you and I heard your pain. I think I have loved you since that moment. I wept for you. Are you angry with me?"

He took a moment before answering, but then he shook his head. "Sophie," he said, "I am not so experienced with women that I know much about these matters, but as we are confessing sins...you were not a maid before this, were you?"

I felt the blood drain from my face. I couldn't answer. His words had conjured up that other hated face. I turned away, hoping to dispel the memories with the slight shaking of my head. A tear spilled down my cheek and I pressed my face into the cushion to get rid of the evidence of it. Damn.

Eric sat up in alarm and rolling me over, he looked down in my face and traced the path my tear had taken with a fingertip. "Sophie? Sophie. How did you come to be at the opera house in the first place? Sophie." His voice had grown somewhat dark with suspicion.

I shook my head, "It was just better that I come here. Does it matter so much? Does it make a difference?" I did not want to answer. I was afraid of what he might do if he knew the answer.

He took me back in his arms, "No, of course it does not matter. You are mine now."

I wrapped my arms around his neck and kissed him hard. I felt the stirrings of his wanting and my own again and abandoned all thoughts, letting his love wash away the dark memories of that other life.

She slept. That was good, she was exhausted. He was tired too, admittedly, but there was something that needed to be done before he could rest, and it was best he do so while she was asleep. They would leave in the morning, this errand could not wait.

He looked at her lying there against his pillows, that impossible pile of thick straight hair colored like a lion's mane spread out in a tangled mess. The temptation to knot it around his fingers once again was strong, but he resisted. He penned a brief note to her and left it on the table, with a bottle of wine and some bread and fruit in case she woke.

Fitting his mask carefully into place, and wrapping his cloak and hood around him, he quietly slid back the door and went out, leaving the door partly open so as not to wake her with the sound of its closing.

The Phantom of the Opera had one last task to perform.

Traveling the rooftops of the ninth arrondissement, he made his way like a shadow through the Paris night to the house of her employer. Swinging from a casement he startled a sleeping pigeon from its nest and it flew away to land yards from him in a squawking huff.

"My apologies, Madame Bird," he said, and made a small bow to it, and kept moving.

Once on the roof of the Gaudet home he made his way carefully to the ground and went immediately to the same window he'd used earlier in the evening. The window was unlatched just as before. Really, it was alarmingly ridiculous how naive people were about the security of their own homes. He slipped silently along corridors and stairwells until he was on what he assumed to be the servants' level at the top of the house. With skill born from long years of practice, he silently opened doors and peered into rooms until he found the one he was looking for. Slipping in, he closed the door behind, turned the lock and went to the bed.

The young man sleeping there looked younger in sleep, his face relaxed and open, that damned hair falling over his cheeks. So like his Sophie, he thought.

In one swift move he knelt with one knee on the bed, grabbed the young man and put a hand over his mouth.

The man's eyes flew open and he struggled, wide eyed panic in his face. The Phantom had the advantages of surprise, strength and skill though and he just held him like a bear. After a time the man's struggles lessened enough for The Phantom to think he might be able to focus on spoken words.

"Stop struggling. I don't mean to hurt you. I am here on behalf of Sophie, and did not want you shouting to bring the

household running. Do you understand?" He had to repeat himself one more time for the words to sink in, but when they did, the young man nodded.

"I assure you, if you shout out when I remove my hand, I can break your neck and be gone before anyone even realizes what room the sound came from. Your word that you will be silent? For Sophie's sake, I'd not harm you."

Another nod and The Phantom removed his hand from the man's mouth.

They faced off against one another for a moment before the young man said, "You are the Phantom of the Opera, aren't you?"

The Phantom nodded, "So they have called me. You are Henri, Sophie's cousin?"

Henri nodded in his turn. "Where is she? Is she all right?"

"She is well. She is asleep and does not know I am here. I do not think she would have allowed this visit had she known."

"You mean this?"

"I swear it. I intend to marry her."

"And you believe you are a suitable match for my cousin? You? A hunted man?" Henri asked aggressively.

No, actually, The Phantom thought, I don't. He shook his head a little. "Does it matter at this point if it is suitable or not? The damage is already done to her reputation. And she is...mine."

"Your actions, sir, are not those of a gentleman!"

"Then it is a fine thing I do not consider myself such. Assure yourself, I will give my life for her. I will take her where she will be safe. She will want for nothing as long as I live and I will see to it that she wants for nothing after I am gone as well. "

Another facing off as each man took the other's measure and Henri gauged the sincerity in The Phantom's words.

A decision reached, Henri said, "You should know the Gendarmerie have been here to question me. My employer went straight to them after your appearance this night."

The Phantom nodded, absorbing this information. He expected that to be the case. The second half of his errand would have to be swift then.

"So why have you come here?" Henri finally asked. "It could hardly be to ask my permission for her hand. You've already taken her."

"I want information. She has been badly hurt. I want to know how and by whom."

"She has not told you herself?"

"Sophie is very clever. I am sure she knew what I would do should she tell me. She is concerned for my soul," he said dryly.

"And you are not?" asked Henri.

"Monsieur, my soul is already damned beyond saving. But my ego can be satisfied by destroying the man who has hurt her. It will have to suffice"

Henri stood from the bed and wrapped a coat around himself. "It gets damned cold up here when the fire goes out, and I do not feel up to this conversation sitting in my bed," he said, then he sighed. "You have guessed that my family was not always of the serving class? Yes? Well then, we were a family of successful merchants. Two brothers: Sophie's father and my own. Sophie was educated by a governess and raised to marry well, if not exactly noble. She would have been well placed. Myself too, for that matter. Our fathers' ship went down, my father was on it, and he perished. Sophie's father was not, but he had an apoplexy at the news and died soon after. Our families' fortunes were drastically changed. Sophie was 10. I was 18. We were forced to sell most of what we owned, and I went to work as a valet as soon as I could find a position. My background helped secure me this place here. At first, my mother and Sophie's combined the households into one, selling only our own. But it was not enough to settle the debt left by the sinking of our fortune. The house Sophie was born in was sold to my Father's largest competitor. I think he found it amusing to be living in the home of his rivals. He also found it amusing to allow our mothers to stay on in the house. He was frequently gone on business trips and was unmarried. It was convenient, I suppose, to make housekeepers of a sort out of them.

I was gone by that time, but I have heard the stories. The man was -is- a wretched blackguard. He forced himself on Sophie. It started when she was only 11 and went on for more than a year! When she at last confided in her mother, she was sent to me here. It was the only way we could protect her. Our mothers still live in the house. There is nothing they can do. If we report him, Sophie's reputation is ruined and they will surely be turned out."

Eric's mood was darkening, though he had known it must be something like this. But to have been so young! "Has he harmed them as well?" Eric asked.

Henri shook his head, "It seems his perversions only run to young girls. He has not touched them, not as far as I know anyway, and I have asked and asked. I would have done something had I thought they had. I'm not sure what, my salary here is...well I would have done something."

"So she came to work at the opera house?" Eric prodded.

"Yes, the Gaudet's are great supporters of the opera, and I used this to beg her a position in the costume department as a seamstress. She had learned to sew well as a child, you see."

The Phantom paced once across the tiny room and then turned, "Where can I find this man?"

"You are going to kill him?"

"No. I would not compromise your mothers' positions again. I mean to avenge Sophie and make certain he will never again hurt anyone."

The next part of his errand did not take long. He stole a horse from a nearby sleeping livery and quickly made his way to the address Henri had given him. It was a mere half an hour to scout the house, find his way in, discover the room where his prey slept, wake the man and confirm that he was indeed the perpetrator of the crimes against Sophie and heaven knew how many other girls. Five minutes more and the cad was unmanned and tied to his bed, one hand tied between his legs, pressing the wad of his own nightshirt to the wound The Phantom had dealt him. The man had screamed, but as there was a gag in his mouth only a muffled squeaking had broken the stillness.

"Keep the pressure on that," The Phantom said, "I would not have you bleeding to death. I wish you to live with the knowledge of what you have done and what you will never again be able to do."

The Phantom moved to the window. "Do not fear, they will find you soon, I will arrange it."

More muffled cries and The Phantom was out the window and down to the ground. He untied his stolen horse, led it to the front door of the house, closed off from the street by a walled courtyard, and broke open the door with a carefully placed kick of his boot. The horse shied at this, but The Phantom held fast and it quieted in his grip. Less than a minute to lead the horse into the vestibule and remove it's bridle and saddle, and then out the door he went, shutting it behind him.

He waited in shadow a moment, listening, hearing the occasional clop turn into a crash as the horse knocked something over, then grow into a veritable cacophony as it spooked itself and started thrashing around the house. When he heard the first sounds of human voices enter the fray, he nodded satisfied and left the premises entirely. The servants would surely wish to alert the Master of the household about this, and would find him trussed and gelded.

Catching a free ride on top of a brougham he spotted heading in his general direction he hurried back to the Opera House. The Phantom's job was done. Now Eric could rest with his Sophie before moving on.

Ten

I woke stretching like a cat. I felt delicious. I wasn't sure why for a second, but then remembered everything and turned. The bed was empty beside me, so was the room, but I could see wine and food left on a table so got up to look for a note. My thighs felt wonderfully achy as I moved across the room. I smiled remembering why. Sure enough there was a note on the table. He just said he had to go on an errand and would return shortly.

I rinsed my mouth with wine and spat it out in the chamber pot. Then I used this item for its intended purpose, covered it and set it outside the door to one side, not at all sure what to do with it from there. I decided Eric must surely have a system in place and he could answer those types of questions when he returned.

I dressed in my petticoats and chemise, lacing my corset up very loosely for comfort, and slipping my stockings on. I could not be bothered with the skirts or boots. I ate some grapes, a few bites of bread, sipped some wine. I went to the door and poked my head out, no Eric. Unsure what to do with myself and not wanting to leave, I moved through the room, deciding to explore my immediate surroundings. Behind the screen were some pegs driven into the stone wall. On these hung garments: a dressing gown, frock coat, a shirt or two. In the trunk by the foot of the bed were stacks and stacks of papers of all kinds, drawings, written texts, diagrams, musical scores; all stacked and tied neatly. A cabinet by the table held more food, and dishes and spare candles. On the desk was the trunk he had taken from deep in the armoire the night before, the trunk from which he had gotten the ring I still wore on my thumb.

It was standing open. I looked in. It was filled with jewels of obvious value and coins, so many coins, a veritable fortune of coins and stones! French coins, certainly, but also coins I did not recognize. Coins from a world I had never explored, and jewelry from those other lands too. My mouth dropped open as I explored the realms of this trunk. The Phantom of the Opera was very wealthy! I had not truly realized that until this moment. I had thought, when I thought of it at all, that he survived off what he gleaned from the Opera House.

I shut the lid of the trunk. With nothing else to do but await Eric's return, I pulled a book from the shelf and crawled back onto the bed with it and the bottle of wine. Curling up, I opened the book on my lap and began to read.

I was happily encamped here when I heard a noise.

I smiled, thinking it was Eric returning. I went to the door and listened. My smile faded. This was more than one person. This was many, many people, and they were taking no pains to conceal their movements. They were coming this way. They must be hunting for Eric. Did they already know of the existence of this apartment? Would they find it if they did not? Certainly they were headed this direction. What should I do? Should I hole up and hope they passed me by, or should I flee and hope I could evade them? A moment's thought and I had decided. I'd run. I knew these tunnels better than anyone, save Eric. My best hope was flight.

I dashed back into the room, straight to the chest of coins and jewels. I was absolutely not going to leave that for marauders to find! I slammed the lid and latched it, then picked it up. Or tried to pick it up. The blasted thing was too heavy for me. I'd never get far with it! All right then, it must be hidden and hope for the best. I pushed it to the edge of the table, and with all my strength, wrapped my arms about it and heaved. It dropped like a brick to the floor, but with my arms about it, stayed upright. I pushed it hard as I could and it slid one agonizing inch at as time across the stone floor towards the armoire. With nowhere else obvious occurring to me to hide it, I thought the armoire was my best bet. Perhaps Eric, in his uncanny wisdom, had built a secret compartment into the back of it, or something.

As it happened, I was right, Eric had indeed built a secret compartment, but it was in the armoire's floor and was conveniently open when I finally reached it, shoving my burden ahead of me. Somehow, with the strength of desperation fueling my efforts, I got one corner of the thing up into the armoire's base, then the other three, and shoved it towards the opening in the floor of the armoire. It landed on its side within, but the latch stayed strong, so I left it that way. It was down about 3 feet. There were two layers of hidden door above it, and I closed the first, then ran and grabbed as much silverware as I could find and dropped that in there. Perhaps it would stop anyone from looking further if they did find the hidden compartment. I closed the second door, rolled the fabric back over it that had been pushed to one side but was clearly meant to conceal any trace of the door, and then spread shoes over that. That was the best I could do, it would have to be enough.

The raised voices and footsteps were growing closer. Good God, it sounded like a veritable mob out there. I wondered if they had pitchforks and hanging nooses. What would they do if they found me? I rushed to my discarded skirts and blouse. I hadn't time, I thought. I snatched my wrap from the floor and threw it about my shoulders. Then I grabbed the other clothes and made for the door.

I was too late. Eric's apartment was at the end of a passage. It was 30 or 40 feet to the nearest junction and the first of the mob was already there. The firelight from their torches threw their faces into murderous, devilish relief. They appeared like demons come to claim me and take me to hell. I felt faint. There was nowhere to go but back, so I did. I backed into the room and rolled the door as quickly as I could. It was no good, it was so heavy, I couldn't get it shut fast enough and a torch shoved its way through the gap and stopped it from sealing.

"Whore!" I heard from beyond. "Devil's mistress!"

The door slowly rolled back. This was it then, there would be no quarter shown, I was sure. They were too enraged. I would die here, and possibly suffer worse beforehand. I felt terrified but strangely calm, like a prisoner going to the hangman's noose. I would die, but at least they would not get Eric if they hadn't already.

The first few men through the door advanced towards me. They were still shouting, and more were pressing through the narrow opening. A dismayed cry from just outside the stone door gave me momentary pleasure. Someone must have inadvertently tripped over the chamber pot. I wickedly wished them well of it, then snatched up a heavy candlestick holder. I was detached and calculating. How many could I club before they took me? Two? Three perhaps? I backed to the far side of the room. I would die, but I would fight first.

"Sophie, get down!" I heard his voice, the beloved voice, echo through the chamber. I knew not where it came from, but I didn't wait to find out. I threw myself to the floor beyond the bed and a second later the massive mirror plummeted to the stone floor sending shards of razor like glass hurling throughout the room. I covered my face, and felt pinpricks of pain driving into my feet and legs where they stuck out from the back of the bed. Nothing serious, I thought, just stings. The attackers were not so lucky. There were so many of them pressed against the door, that the first ones had nowhere to go and were impaled by hurling shards of glass. I heard cries of pain and fear. I chanced a look up and saw an opening in the stone behind where the mirror had stood. Eric was flying through the room towards me.

The next instant I was snatched up by his arm about my waist and pressed to his side.

"Hold on to me!" he shouted, and threw something to the ground. A noxious yellow cloud rose around us, shielding us from the view of the attackers. I coughed but clung to Eric like a burr. He took a step back and pulled one of the ropes from the blue velvet hangings. He tugged it hard and kicked what looked to me like a doorstop on the floor. Suddenly we shot upwards towards the stone ceiling, Eric holding the rope tightly wound around one wrist, his other arm about me. Another of his wonderful trap doors dropped open in the ceiling above our heads and we shot through like an arrow.

We landed on the next floor up. I could hear coughing and cries coming from below. Eric pulled the door shut and pulled his sword from its sheath at his waist, cutting the rope. Then he grabbed my hand and we flew down the corridor. I grieved the loss of my gloves and skirts, left behind in the escape, but was glad of my wrap, still firmly wrapped around my shoulders. I pulled it closer as we ran. It seemed an age we ran, down one stone corridor after another. I scarcely knew were we were anymore, only a vague idea of what part of the Opera House might be above us. I could still hear the shouting of the mob we had left behind. The miracles of the acoustics in this great house kept their angry shouts and screams echoing all around us.

We came at last to the edge of the lake. I could see Eric's old chambers across it. I thought perhaps that was where were heading, but no. We ran around the edge of the lake, through more corridors and at last came to the underground canals we had followed one day in his boat.

"Can you swim if need be?" he turned and asked me, not slowing.

I nodded. I was not a strong swimmer, and had not had the opportunity to do any swimming at all in many years, but one was not born to a merchant who was on the sea half their lives without at least being able to paddle about. I thought it was not a skill one lost over time.

At my nod, Eric made a decision and we charged into the canals. We waded through tunnel after tunnel of water. We climbed from the water whenever there was a dry ledge running along and used that to make our retreat faster and easier, but eventually we would have to plunge back into the water, most of it no more than knee deep, but some as deep as my waist and very cold. I lifted my petticoats as high as I could to make ploughing through the water less of a task, but I was growing tired. It was hard going. Eric never let go my hand, and as I began to flag, he put an arm about my waist and bore my weight to make the going easier for me. I sagged against him and just concentrated on moving my legs, one frozen foot in front of the other, and another and yet another. Keep going, Sophie, I urged myself. Just keep going. The shouting of the mob was a spur in my side and kept me moving. I didn't know if they were following us or if we could just still hear them, but at last it seemed that their voices grew fainter and fainter and I allowed myself to believe that maybe we had begun to leave them behind. Eric drove us onwards however, taking no chance.

At last we came to a part of the canals I recognized, there was the ledge and there the door to the bridge across the Seine. I belatedly wondered what had happened to the boat. Eric climbed out and reached a hand to me. I grasped it and he pulled me, shivering and grateful, from the water. We made our way along the ledge to the door. Opening it, Eric helped me through and followed behind. Taking a quick glance about, we saw no one walking the quay in this still dark early morning so we jumped down from the little ledge and turned to walk down the quay and then to freedom. I had no idea where we would go and I didn't much care, I just followed Eric.

Two steps only we took and a shadow moved out from behind the bridge abutment where he had hidden. I felt Eric's hand go to his sword again in its sheath.

"I thought you might be coming this way," the shadow said.

Inspector Bruyere. I froze. Eric besides me hummed with tension, but said nothing. The predator was prowling again. I could feel it in him, like watching a werewolf change with the full moon.

The Inspector shrugged apologetically, "The maps, I'm afraid. They laid it out quite clearly. I take it you managed to evade the crowd that went below? I thought you might. Not so easy to catch on your own ground! But out here, it is another matter, I think. So glad to know my instincts are still so sound," the figure said, and then, "And Mademoiselle! It is indeed a pleasure to find you here as well!"

"Not for me, I assure you," I said. There went my tongue again.

Inspector Bruyere laughed then addressed Eric again. "Your little appearance at the home of Monsieur Gaudet this evening did not go unreported. Did you expect it would?"

I glanced sharply at Eric. What was this?

"Oh, you didn't know, Mademoiselle? Yes, your escort here decided to threaten your previous employer this evening." his attention shifted back to Eric. "And then of course, we found the man Armand badly beaten. He was raving about a monster with a mask. One does put two and two together and comes up with you yet again, doesn't one?"

Eric had adjusted his weight, moving me slightly behind him and now he pushed me back and let me go. His hand gripped his sword hilt and it slid, singing, out of its sheath. I jumped back and hugged the abutment of the bridge. The Inspector pulled his sword a mere second after Eric, and the two men assumed fighting stances.

"You may come across a third part of the equation eventually. If he dares to come forward," Eric said dryly, obviously taunting The Inspector with his lack of information.

Again I looked at Eric, finding myself distinctly curious about tonight's "errand". I was going to have to ask at some point, I thought inanely and then The Inspector lunged. I knew nothing of sword fighting, I still do not, so I can't tell you what moves they used or what the classical terminology of the feints and parries would be. I just know it was not a fight to satisfy honor with a little drawing of blood. This was a fight to the death. I stood terrified and not a little ashamed at my utter lack of ability to help in any way. I was useless, the only assistance I could be was to stay out of the way and not add an additional burden for Eric in this battle.

Eric moved up the bank a foot or two, adding extra height to his already taller advantage. He lashed down at the Inspector, but the Inspector was skilled. He ducked the blow and swung his own sword up at Eric's midsection. A quick shift and parry from Eric saved him from being sawn through, but he did receive a slice to his rib cage that must have stung like blazes. I gasped, but tried to stifle my cries so as not to distract Eric from the fight. The wound only served to release the predator even further, and Eric leapt down from his higher ground, bringing his sword down from above in a blow that would have cleaved through the Inspector's shoulder to his heart. The Inspector barely ducked this blow, somehow managed to regain his footing somewhat and responded with an offensive attack of his own. Back and forth the two men went, each dealing the other minor blows, blood blossoming on the shirt fronts of both men. The sound of each blow and animal grunts of the men echoed off the undercarriage of the great bridge we were under.

I scrambled out of the way yet again as the fight moved my direction, clambering further up the embankment, clods of earth rolling down as my feet dislodged them. The Inspector ducked briefly and grabbed one of these, flinging it up into Eric's face in an effort to blind him. Eric whipped his head round so the earth merely glanced off his mask and fell harmlessly to the side, missing the eyes it was intended for. It served the purpose of diverting Eric's deadly attention however, and the Inspector took advantage of the momentary distraction he'd gained and snatched at my retreating ankles. Simultaneously hauling me down the embankment and himself up it besides me, he pulled us to our feet and held me in front of him. Eric stilled, breathing hard, as he watched The Inspector grip my arm and haul me in close to his side. I struggled but it was, of course, no use.

"Turn yourself in to me, and she goes free," The Inspector said. "Do not, and she goes to prison in your stead."

Eric's sword arm dropped at once, and he let go the weapon. I could see calculations and ideas flashing through his brain and being discarded in an instant. Out here, escape was not as easy. The Inspector had been right.

There was nothing for it, then, I was going to have to do something. I only hoped it would help and not hurt us. I casually lifted my knee as high as it would go, turned my toes up and stomped with all my might on the instep of The Inspector's right foot with my heel.

The move would have been more effective on his leather boots had I been wearing my own boots with their little heels, but it seemed it was enough. I doubt it hurt him overly much, but it was an attack from so completely unexpected a corner that he dropped his grip and hopped a few inches. A second later he was reaching for me again, but I had dashed away as fast as I could and was not in easy reach.

Eric was on him in an instant, but he no longer had his own weapon. He drove a fist into The Inspectors face and The

Inspectors head flew sideways, but he brought his own sword up and swung wildly, forcing Eric to step away.

The Inspector drove Eric back, back and farther back, attempting to drive him away from where Eric's sword lay. Eric's feet scrambled beneath him as he sought to regain his control and find some sort of weapon. I worked my own way closer to the discarded sword. The Inspector backed Eric up to the wall of the bridge, and still he harried him without pause, each blow coming faster and faster till I could see Eric was struggling to evade each one. With a sudden twist of his body, Eric spun away into a brief opening on the right, coming around almost behind the Inspector and forcing that other man off his balance slightly. It gave Eric the pause he needed to regain the sword I'd slid across the ground to him and he drove the inspector back the way they'd come.

Waiting for the moment when he could get through the Inspector's sword, Eric, with a murderous yell, launched himself at the Inspector, landing on him in a tangle of arms, legs and swords. The Inspector went down like a stone under Eric's superior weight, his sword skittering across the ground to stop a few feet from his grasp. I ran to it and shoved it away. The two men thrashed on the ground, Eric with a hand on The Inspector's throat, the Inspector with both hands on Eric's one, trying to pull him away. Eric was bringing his sword up to bear with his free hand, grasping the hilt and sliding it along the ground with a zinging noise. The Inspector fought with all the strength of the doomed but he was not big enough to shift Eric's weight and the hand at his throat was gradually cutting off the air to his lungs. He was weakening fast. Eric brought up the sword and with a solid blow, slammed the hilt into the man's temple. Inspector Bruyere went limp as a rag. Eric, panting with effort, released him and stood swiftly, swinging the sword in front just in case the other man was feigning unconsciousness. He wasn't. I went to Eric's side, putting a hand on his arm lightly, surreptitiously inspecting the various cuts and bloody areas of his shirt for a mortal wound. There were some worrying ones but none so bad that he would bleed to death. We had won, but the Inspector was starting to moan as the air began to get to his lungs. The blow had not been hard enough to kill. Eric kept his sword point at the man's throat as he awoke.

The Inspector blinked once, then twice, as his eyes focused and he remembered where he was. As he registered the sword above him and the man holding it he said, "Go on; kill me then, you murderous wretch."

"No, I don't think I shall, for my lady's sake. She doesn't like it," Eric said. "But I hope you can swim."

And with that, Eric bent down, lifted the man by the shirt front and flung him off the stone wall and into the Seine.

The Inspector landed on his back with an enormous splash that peppered us with droplets of water. He flailed madly as he tried to gain control of himself in the thickly flowing water. He could swim, after all, but not terribly well. It would most likely keep him alive though, long enough to find a landing place and pull himself out. We watched for a few moments as he swore at us, trying to shuck out of his coat which must be threatening to pull him under, while the current carried him away from us.

I could not resist a little wave and smile and an, "*Au revoir*!" as he was pulled inexorably downstream. Eric looked down at me and while he could not exactly smile with the predator still on him, still there was an amused shift in his stance at my remark. I was learning to read him well.

"We must go. Quickly," he said and pulled me upstream. We ran.

Several hundred yards up the river was a small dock with perhaps a dozen boats tied down to it. Eric led me there. He chose one seemingly at random and handed me aboard. It was a small craft with a little sail. It took me a moment to recognize it for what it was, that same small vessel from the lake, but fitted to be less conspicuous. Eric loosed the boat and flung the rope to me as he jumped aboard. I caught it and coiled it in the bottom of the boat.

Eric took up the oars and rowed us out into the middle of the Great River then let the current take us downstream. A few minutes later we passed by The Inspector who had made his way to the bank and was struggling to find a handhold and drag himself up. He paid no attention to our small anonymous skiff going by. The sky was just starting to lighten with the faintest touches of indigo, as though a master painter had splashed color along the horizon in a great sweep. On this immense wide river, Eric's mask would go unseen and our passage to whatever destination Eric had planned for us, unmarked. I moved to him standing at the bow and placed a light kiss on one of the wounds on his arm.

He looked down at me and laid that arm round my shoulders, pulling me close. We stood, as our little bateau moved ever onward away from the Opera House, away from all I had known, watching the sun as it rose over the city of Paris, setting the world aflame.

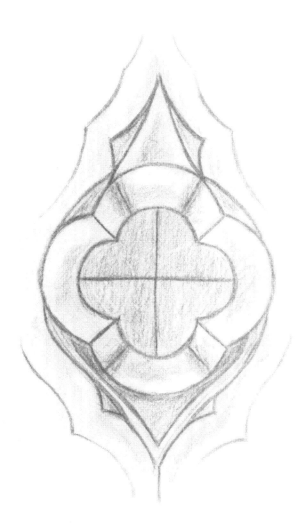

Epilogue

The sun was setting. We stood on the rooftop, amidst the mascarons and quartrefoils, watching the colors of the sky change from blues to oranges, to reds and finally indigos. I was the first to spot tonight's evening star. We took pains each night to see who would be the one to first see that small shining beacon in the early night sky. I pointed it out to Eric with a small cry of glee. He smiled at me, bundled me up in his arms against the chill that was increasing in this winter air and held me, my back to his chest.

A new city. A new theatre, our theatre. A run down immense pallazzo, several blocks off the Plaza San Marco, along the Grand Canal, bought, along with our passage here from Paris, with the money in the chest I'd so painstakingly hidden in the false bottom of the armoire. Henri had very carefully, following Eric's directions down into the cellars, managed to retrieve it for us through the tunnel that lay below Eric's chamber, though he dared not attempt a foray into the room itself for any of our other belongings. Eric was thorough, it must be admitted, and had left no stone overturned, so to speak. He had always planned to have several escape routes both for him and his fortune. He was busy now designing and building them into our current residence though I did my best to convince him it was no longer necessary. Caution had been so long a habit of his life that he could not let it go and he prowled restlessly if he felt too caged. So I left him to it. It made for interesting journeys and discoveries of my own. After all, I could not give up my adventurous side either, and I delighted in finding out his little secrets and sharing my discoveries with him over dinner.

Restoration of the pallazzo and its evolution into a theatre was almost complete. We had developed the theatrical portions first: the stage, orchestra pit, boxes, seats, and backstage areas for example. And rehearsals had been going on for several weeks for our first production, one of Eric's, "Constantine". I was in charge of the costume department, ostensibly, but in reality, left most of the running of it to a very capable costume mistress we had hired, both because I had little patience for much of it, and also because Eric desired me with him making creative decisions and others about the rebuilding of the theatre.

Our apartments in the rear of the palazzo suited us well. We had started with a single room that was in decent repair, but now that much of the work was done, we have moved into our permanent quarters. They are spacious and light and I have filled them with creams and pale golds and blues and bought crate after crate of the sparkling, perfect glass that Venice is so famous for: chandeliers, bowls, goblets of all sizes and shapes and more. I adore it, and I have sent some as a gift back to Henri, and my mother, calling myself Madame D'Oro, the Italian word for gold, which is the name of the palazzo, and the one we adopted when we bought it.

The little scrap of shell from Henri sits on the mantel of our bedroom fireplace cradled in one of these beautiful glass dishes. We leave it with the scarred side facing up most of the time, but when Eric slides into one of his rages and I feel the predator in him, or when I fall into one of my fearful memories of my childhood and become withdrawn and silent, the other one of us will turn the shell up as an unspoken signal to the one in need. Thus we are reminded of the beauty that lies beneath and that is usually all it takes for the darkness to begin to pass.

We are lucky in that our palazzo has a side entrance on the canals as well as the spectacular front entrance on the Grand Canal that our patrons will enter through. This side entrance is our private one and we have a small gondola right outside our door. Eric could not have looked more at home when he first stepped into our new little boat and rowed us silently through the dark narrow canals and high walls of Venice. I knew we had chosen well between the canals and one other very important aspect of Venetian culture.

Venice is a city of masks, with a two month long festival in Winter called Carnivale, and certain aspects of the running of the government requiring its members to wear masks. It took some time for Eric to feel comfortable coming out amongst people, and he still tended to stay out of sight most of the time, but he can wander the streets mostly without being noticed now, especially during this season and after a year here he is starting to do so with more frequency. We plan to open our "Constantine" during this year's Carnivale, starting in two weeks. I suspect he will truly feel at home then, and I am anxious for the festival to begin.

This evening we stood and watched the stars making their debuts one by one, and I cradled my hands across my belly, only now beginning to show the very slightest of roundness, and smiled inwardly. Soon, very soon I would tell him, now that I was sure. Tonight, certainly, before we went downstairs. But for a few more moments I would keep this one last secret to myself and think of the wonderful beauty that lies beneath the surface of us all.

Author's Note

I have to say here a special thank you to Debra Cosentino. A chance conversation led to the creation of this tale, so blame her! And to my buddy Selina Fenech who pointed me on the right path to indie publishing.

Also, many thanks to my very own Phantom, my husband Dean, whose belief in me never wavers, even when it's 2 a.m. and I am insisting he stay awake long enough to hear "just one more chapter, honey." And to my children, who love me enough to say, "Go, Mom!" no matter what I might be spouting off about at the time.

I have taken some liberties in the telling of this story. For one, this story is based on the 1910 novel "The Phantom of the Opera" by Gaston Leroux, not on more contemporary versions of the story. My story, however, does start with a somewhat different ending to the original novel. I needed an empty Opera House, so rather than have every barrel of dynamite The Phantom had set to blow drowned and rendered harmless as in the original story, I had some actually blow up, causing the serious fire we read about in our Prologue . This sympathetic relationship to fire is very gently hinted at throughout my story and it is to be implied that this may be how he received his wounds.

For another, the Carnivale in Venice had largely fallen to the wayside during the 19th century. It had enjoyed popularity from the 12th century through the 18th and it was indeed an approximately two month long festival at that time. It was not revived until 1979, but I thought it was time for Eric to find a place where he could at last feel at home and Venice's Carnivale, along with its canals and theatrical culture suited this purpose perfectly. So I cheated, frankly, and made the cessation of the festival just...go away. I trust the rest of my portrayal of Venice is flattering enough that sticklers will forgive this bending of history to suit my story.

I have created a Paris that would suit Sophie and Eric. The street the Gaudet's home is on does not exist, or at least, if it does, it'd be a rather nifty coincidence, as I made it up as I wrote. The Palais Garnier, which is indeed the Opera House that inspired Gaston Leroux's novel, The Phantom of the Opera, is in the ninth arrondissement, and some of the streets I have mentioned are in fact there, and so is the proximity of the Seine. It was easy to imagine the underground canals leading to this fantastic waterway, but I do not know if they actually do, nor do I know at what time the streets I mentioned were constructed.

I did stick to the terminology, history and facts of the 19th century as well as I might, but in some cases I sacrificed perfect accuracy for a better tale. I take comfort in knowing that M. Leroux's novel was a fantasy as well. I hope he would not be too distressed at my weaving some of my own fantasy into the world he so graciously and beautifully created. Thank you, Mr. Leroux.

About the Author

A professional misfit, Jacqueline has been living in a world of her own creation since she was about 5 years old. An international model and actress in her twenties, she began a fantasy art career in her thirties and soon gathered a worldwide fan base for her images of fairies, unicorns and more enchanted creatures.

She recently opened a vintage shop in her hometown of Burbank, CA that is much like her misfit mind. One never quite knows what one will find there.

Her magical world of Toadstool Farm is also inhabited by her husband, Dean, her two incredible children, six highly opinionated horses, one silly dog, one far too dignified dog, one turtle named Tulip who really doesn't have much to say one way or another, and an ever shifting gathering of Fae Folk.

You can read more about her at her official website: www.toadstoolfarm.com.

She remains a misfit.

CPSIA information can be obtained at www.ICGtesting.com
Printed in the USA
LVOW06s2253130414

381561LV00008B/116/P